T0267836

BREATHING UNDERWATER

BREATHING UNDERWATER

ABBEY LEE NASH

HOLIDAY HOUSE • NEW YORK

HOLIDAY HOUSE is registered in the U.S. Patent and Trademark Office.

Printed and bound in January 2024 at Maple Press, York, PA, USA.

www.holidayhouse.com

First Edition

1 3 5 7 9 10 8 6 4 2

Library of Congress Cataloging-in-Publication Data is available.

ISBN: 978-0-8234-5386-3 (hardcover)

FOR MY
GRANDMOTHER,
WHO TAUGHT ME THAT
LIFE IS UNCERTAIN AND
WRITING WILL CARRY
ME THROUGH.

CHAPTER
ONE

If adrenaline is the body's fight-or-flight response, then every time I race, I'm fighting for my life. Instead of fear, there's lightning in my veins—and I'm addicted.

Perched now on the starting block, my pulse throbs in my throat as my toes find purchase on the rough surface. The girls in the previous heat thrash through the water beneath me, their arms and legs churning up froth, their fingers reaching for the win only one of them will find.

At the whistle, I drop low, mentally blocking out the swimmers in my periphery, the excited din of the crowd. It's only the water and me. When the starter buzzes, I fly.

Though I sense the other swimmers nearby, crashing down their lanes like hungry sharks, I'm lost in a world where nothing matters but the precision of my stroke, the speed of my turns, and the win.

Inhale, exhale.

Reach, pull.

I press my palm against the touchpad and break the surface, chest heaving with exhaustion and relief. In the stands, my dad pumps the air with an exuberant fist. It's only one race at the beginning of a summer that will hold many, but with Nationals in August and a college scholarship to secure, every win matters. Even a few added seconds can mean shattered dreams.

—

"You killed it out there today," my best friend, Mac, says later in the locker room as we strip out of our wet suits and change back into street clothes.

"You too," I tell her. Mac's a sprinter. Though I'm one of the fastest on our team in distance events, she can kick my ass in the 50-meter free any day.

"So much for feeling off."

"I was just a little run-down." The last few weeks have been a hamster wheel of two-a-day practices and studying for final exams. This morning, I would have much rather spent the first Saturday of summer relaxing behind a book than powering through an all-day meet. But no matter how tired I am, swimming is where I feel fully alive, my lungs fully expanded. It's in the rest of my life that I'm holding my breath.

"So tonight—" Mac starts.

"I'm thinking burrito bowls and a rom-com marathon?"

Mac slides on her flip-flops and slings her backpack over one shoulder. "Actually, Rachel invited me to sleep over."

"Rachel?" A distance swimmer like me, Rachel is my fiercest competition on the team; tonight, I edged her out by mere milliseconds. Until this year, Mac's never seemed to care much for Rachel or her rich, snooty squad. She and I have been basically inseparable since middle school, when my grades earned me a scholarship to Oakwood Academy. But ever since Seth King asked Mac to prom last month, she's suddenly cool by association, despite her ancient Corolla and outlet mall wardrobe.

2

"God, Tess. Do you think you could sound any less disgusted?" Mac asks.

"Doubt it."

"I was hoping you'd come, too."

I stare at her. "Did you see the way Rachel looked at me after I beat her in the 200? Pretty sure I'm not on the invite list."

Mac glances over my shoulder. I follow her gaze to see Rachel brushing her hair in the mirror, flanked by her usual sidekicks, Lily and Simone. "Hey, Rach," Mac calls.

Rachel looks at us, her brush still moving methodically through her chin-length black hair.

"It's cool if Tess comes tonight, too, right?"

"Um." Rachel's eyes assess me like a worn-out sweater she's trying to decide whether to donate or throw out. Either way, she doesn't want it in her closet. "Sure. I guess."

"See?" Mac says to me. "You're invited."

I snort.

"Please," Mac says, dropping her voice below the other girls' hearing range. "We always do what you want to do. It's the first night of summer vacation, and I just want to have fun."

That stings a little—since when is a rom-com marathon *not* Mackenzie's idea of fun?

I sigh. "Fine."

Mac grabs my face and gives me a noisy kiss on the cheek, earning an eyebrow raise from the girls at the mirror. We head out of the locker room to the parking lot, where the evening sky is painted in pastel.

"I have a feeling about this summer," says Mac. "It's going to be a good one."

With tonight's win still thumping against my chest, I couldn't agree more.

"Pizza's here!" Rachel's mom calls from the top of the basement steps.

"Not it," says Rachel, pressing her finger to the side of her nose, just ahead of Lily and Simone. Rachel smiles at me, sugar-sweet. "Tess? Would you mind?"

Mac casts me a guilty glance. "I'll get it," she says, starting to stand.

"It's fine," I tell her. Any excuse to escape the claustrophobic tangle of pillows and blankets and the monster shark movie that would make even seasoned swimmers like us swear off open water for good.

"Hurry up," Lily says, pausing the movie as an unsuspecting diver's blood floods the screen. "This is the best part."

Upstairs, Mrs. Kolowski is stacking paper plates and napkins on top of two pizza boxes. Her purse-sized designer dogs circle her ankles, yapping. "I would've thought they'd stop delivering after eleven."

"I guess not," I say, sliding the food off the counter.

"Tell Rachel I'm going to bed. You girls try to keep it down, okay?"

The basement's quiet when I head back down the stairs; four pairs of eyes, including Mac's, skirt away from mine. "What's up?" I say casually, putting the pizza on the glass-topped coffee table. Lily and Simone dive-bomb the food like starving seagulls.

"There's a party at the tracks," Rachel says. "We want to go." Her eyes narrow, predatory. "You know, if you're comfortable with that."

Shrouded by woods, the long-abandoned section of train track by the creek offers a semi-private place to party, but getting busted there is practically a rite of passage in Oakwood. That could do some serious damage to my squeaky-clean record and maybe even compromise my Oakwood scholarship. "My parents would literally kill me if they found out."

"I told you," Mac mutters. "Let's just stay here, okay?"

Simone ignores her. "Who says they're going to find out?"

"Yeah, c'mon, Tess," Lily chimes in over a cheesy mouthful. "Live a little."

"How about we decide with a friendly competition?" Rachel suggests.

Competition is to me as *Seth* is to Mac. "What'd you have in mind?"

"You and me, outside. End of the pool and back. Twice. Winner decides what we're doing with the rest of our night."

"You want to race me? I thought you *wanted* to go out tonight."

"Damn," Lily breathes.

Rachel's eyes flash. "That's pretty confident from somebody who only beat me today by half a second. Anything could happen at Nationals."

Suddenly the competition Rachel's suggesting doesn't seem so friendly. She's hungry, and she's got something to prove.

"Can't we just do, like, rock paper scissors or something?" Mac suggests weakly.

But it's too late. Rachel has dangled the proverbial carrot, and I can already taste it.

"You're on."

We scurry like giggling mice up the basement stairs and through the darkened kitchen. Rachel quietly unlatches the sliding glass door. The pool lights make the blue water look an eerie yellowish-green. A cool nighttime breeze rustles through my pajamas, raising goosebumps on my pale skin. The backyard is surrounded by a wooden privacy fence, but the nearby houses are close enough that anyone looking through the upstairs windows can see over the fence. God, I hope her neighbors aren't night owls.

Rachel and I slip out of our pajamas. The water is heated, but it still shocks my sleepy skin. I duck under, dodging the splash as Rachel takes the plunge.

"What stroke?" I ask.

Rachel hovers just above the surface of the water, chin submerged. Her words skip like stones. "Underwater. If you come up to breathe, you lose."

Underwater training is supposed to increase endurance, prepare us for the pain we'll be in during a race, but when Coach puts the tarp over the pool to keep us from coming up for air, I swear I can hear the other swimmers struggling. I tip my chin, spitting chlorine. "Fine."

We set it up—one girl at each end of the pool in lieu of a stopwatch. I grip the pool's slippery tile surround, purposefully hyperventilating to release the CO_2 in my lungs and keep myself from needing to breathe.

"Three...two...one!" Simone shouts.

We duck under.

In seconds, my fingers brush the end of the pool, and I turn. I don't have goggles, so I can't really see. Bubbles brush my face and I hear the whoosh of water as Rachel turns behind me.

I pick up my pace and make the second turn with ease. Back and forth—two laps, three—until my chest begins to call for air. On the fourth lap, Rachel closes in behind me, and though my lungs burn, I push harder.

I am the water.

And then everything goes black, and I am nothing at all.

CHAPTER
TWO

I swim slowly to the surface of my consciousness, where faces blur and voices itch my brain like a mosquito bite I can't quite scratch.

"She's awake!"

"Oh, thank God!"

Someone's crying. Why are they crying?

The faces slowly come into focus.

Mac and Rachel, wrapped in towels, cling to each other. Rachel's dad's pants are wet; he keeps crossing and uncrossing his arms. The other girls huddle together, their faces streaked with tears.

I'm lying on the concrete patio, in the center of a circle of worry.

"What—" I try to speak, but my words sound thick and muffled, like there are cotton balls stuffed in the back of my mouth.

A man in a black uniform hovers over me, gray stalks of short hair surrounding a brown mountain of bald. "Tess," he booms. "Can you hear me? Do you know where you are?"

Words float just out of reach, and I panic.

"It's okay," the man says. "You've had a seizure, but your friends here kept you afloat. We're going to take you to the hospital and get you checked out. Everything's going to be okay."

In his eyes, I see the same doubt that floods my chest with fear: everything might not be okay.

———

I've only been to the hospital one other time. In second grade, Timmy Martin said he didn't think I could hang upside down on the monkey bars for five minutes. Turns out he was right, and I got a sprained wrist to prove it. But that was just a trip to the ER and a sling—plus Timmy felt so guilty, he gave me his dessert for the rest of the school year. Not bad when you think about it. Nothing like this.

My parents are waiting for me at the ER. They're both in their pajamas. Mom's lips are white, her eyes swollen behind her glasses, and I start crying as soon as I see her, even though my throat is already burning and my head throbs.

"It's going to be okay, kid," Dad says, squeezing my hand as he walks alongside the stretcher, his slippers squeaking on the freshly bleached floor.

The EMTs wheel me into a curtained room. On the count of three, they hoist me onto the hospital bed, using the sheet underneath me for leverage. That's when I realize I'm basically naked in only my underwear, covered by a damp towel and a few thin blankets.

My arm hurts from the IV they placed during the ambulance ride; rust-colored splatters show underneath the foggy tape. Mom and a kind-eyed nurse help me into a hospital gown while Dad stands sentinel outside the curtain. My legs are trembling, and I don't know if it's because I'm cold or afraid. Maybe it's a little of both.

The night is a blur of blood tests and scans, including one

where they glue electrodes on my scalp and flash lights in my face. It's almost dawn by the time they admit me to the hospital and only then do I give in to my exhaustion, tumbling into a fearful, restless sleep.

———

I've learned three things about this hospital in the few hours since I've been awake:

1. It has terrible cell phone reception. I keep trying to text Mac to let her know I'm okay, but nothing's going through.
2. The cable is crap.
3. The food is revolting.

Thank goodness for Dad, who went on a fast-food mission while Mom and I wait for test results. The neurologist is supposed to come by today, too. So far, everything has looked normal—like my seizure was just some kind of freak occurrence. In the light of day, with the TV on and Mom drinking coffee while she chats on the hospital phone with my sister, last night feels far away, like it happened to dream-me.

"Okay, honey, have a good day," Mom says into the phone. "I will." She hangs up, then walks over to my bed and kisses me on the forehead. "That's from Ali. She said she'll try to come down soon."

My sister, Ali, is five years older than me. She lives in New York City, auditioning by day and waitressing by night. She rarely comes home, and I rarely see her.

"Anybody here order a number seven?" Dad's broad frame fills the doorway, one arm holding a brown paper bag from Paprika and the other a cardboard carrier full of sodas and an iced coffee

I sure hope is mine. He's changed into a T-shirt and jeans and his ever-present knee brace, a holdover of his college football injury. A duffel bag is slung over his shoulder.

"Oh, thank goodness," Mom says, heading straight for the duffel. "I feel so awkward meeting all these hospital people in my jammies."

Dad puts down the food. "I found this one wandering in the lobby," he says as Mac steps into the room. She takes one look at me and bursts into tears.

And then I'm crying because last night did happen, and I'm here in this stupid bed with this stupid gown on, and these stupid wires attached to my arm and chest. I scoot over to make space on the bed, and Mac crawls across, tucking in beside me.

My parents step into the hallway, and then it's just me and Mac, the way it's always been, the way it's supposed to be.

———

"I was so scared." Mac dips another greasy chip into the plastic tub of guacamole propped on my thigh.

"Me too." I sip my coffee, unsure if I want to hear the answer to my next question. "What happened?"

Between bites, Mac tells me Rachel and I were neck and neck when suddenly my body buckled, and I began to sink, one arm and leg thrashing. "I've never seen a seizure before," she says, "but I knew you were drowning."

Two summers of lifeguard training kicking in, Mac dove in after me while the other girls ran to wake Rachel's parents. "You were so stiff. Even with Rachel's help, I could barely keep your face out of the water."

I lean my head on Mac's shoulder. Tears splash on my cheek, and I don't know if they're Mac's or mine.

"I'm okay," I tell her, wondering if it's true. "Everything's going to be fine."

We're watching *The Price Is Right* and placing our bids on a stainless-steel stove and fridge combination when Mom comes back into the room. She's wearing the clothes Dad brought for her—a wrinkled T-shirt and work shoes, not sneakers. "The neurologist is here," she says.

"Can't Mac stay?" I ask.

Mom's brows knit together.

"It's okay," Mac says. She scoots to the end of the bed and slides her feet into her flip-flops. "Text me as soon as you get home."

I promise her I will.

A tall doctor steps into the room. "You must be Tess," she says, sticking out her hand to shake mine. "I'm Dr. Desai."

Mom smooths the back of her hair and sits down. Dad hovers beside my bed, one hand on the rail.

Dr. Desai has reviewed my scans and test results. "The good news is that other than the dehydration that showed up in your bloodwork, almost everything else came back perfectly normal," she says.

I want to feel relieved, but when people start with good news, it means bad news is coming. "Almost everything?"

"The results of your EEG do raise a slight concern," Dr. Desai says.

EEG—the test where they glued electrodes to my scalp like some kind of sci-fi torture device.

"That's the one that checks for seizure activity?" Mom asks.

Dr. Desai nods. "The EEG monitors brain wave activity. We're looking for electrical discharges in response to stimuli, like flashing lights and hyperventilation. When we see this type of abnormality on an EEG, we want to do further testing. Often it doesn't mean anything at all, but in some cases, it can be an indication of an underlying seizure disorder."

"Seizure disorder?" Mom's voice is hollow; it echoes in the small room, reverberating in my chest. "Aren't people born with epilepsy?"

"A person can develop epilepsy at any age," Dr. Desai says. "Many people will experience a seizure at some point in their lives and never have another one again. It's very likely that Tess's seizure was due to the combination of hyperventilation and dehydration, even exhaustion. With inconclusive EEG results, however, it would be wise to follow up with a pediatric neurologist for further testing."

"Is there anything else we need to know?" Dad asks.

Dr. Desai glances at me. "After any kind of seizure, state law requires you surrender your driver's license until you're seizure-free for six months."

"Excuse me?" I sit straight up in bed, my gown falling open at the shoulder.

"Six months?" Dad asks. "Doesn't that seem a little extreme?"

"You said yourself it was probably just because I hyperventilated," I say. "What if this whole thing is just a fluke, and I never have another seizure again?"

"After six months seizure-free, the statistical likelihood that you'll have another seizure does decrease significantly," says the doctor. "For now, however, we need to keep you safe."

"Yeah, but how am I supposed to get to practice?" I ask, turning to Dad.

"We'll figure something out," Dad says. "Don't worry about that right now."

"What sport do you play?" Dr. Desai asks.

"I swim."

Pride puffs Dad's chest. "Tess has a full ride to Northern Hills University."

"Will have," I remind him. My heart's been set on Northern Hills ever since sophomore year, when Wes Andrews, the Northern Hills coach, approached me after practice to tell me about the university's swim program. This year, they'd offered me a full scholarship, but I don't sign until the fall.

"Impressive." Dr. Desai pauses, her eyes skirting momentarily away from mine. "Unfortunately, you really want to avoid anything where losing consciousness would be particularly dangerous, at least until you can get further testing done. I hate to say this, but it might be wise to press pause on swimming for a while."

The room around the doctor blurs, but she stands out in sharpened, cartoon color. "Dad?" I say, silently begging him to intervene.

"Tess has Nationals at the end of the summer," he says. "Not swimming isn't really an option here."

"I understand this is difficult news," Dr. Desai says, "but I'm sure we can all agree Tess's safety is the priority right now."

"Of course," Mom says, shooting Dad a cutting look. They've never agreed on anything when it comes to my swimming career. It was Dad who took an early mail delivery shift so he could coach football at the public high school, a gig that helps pay for my gear and traveling expenses. It's Dad who cheers the loudest at every meet. Mom has always worried that the rigor of my practice schedule doesn't leave enough time for studying. I've spent the last three years constructing the Jenga tower of my life with perfect precision that satisfies them both—straight As and a full athletic scholarship. And now, in one careless move, I've knocked the whole thing down.

My eyes fill up and my throat squeezes. Dad puts his hand on my shoulder, but I grit my teeth and shrug him off. Crying in front of people is right up there with second place: the absolute worst.

Dr. Desai's voice is gentle. "Like I said, these are temporary precautions. Let's just focus on getting the follow-up scheduled."

She tells us she'll get my discharge papers together. The look on her face stings almost as much as the blow her news delivered.

It's pity.

CHAPTER THREE

The short walk downstairs to breakfast is slow and achy. I barely slept last night, my mind replaying the past two days over and over. If I'd just been more hydrated or squeezed in a little rest before the party, maybe none of this would've happened. My seizure feels like a bad dream, but it's everything I've ever worked for that's slipping through my fingers like smoke.

The smell of bacon wafts from the kitchen, where I can hear my parents talking.

"I just don't think we need to wait for some doctor to tell us she can get back in the water," Dad says. "We've got Nationals in two months. How's it going to look to Andrews if she can't compete? She could lose her scholarship before she even signs!"

"Which is exactly why she shouldn't be staking her future on a sport in the first place," Mom retorts. "Professional athletics aren't a sure thing. You should know that better than anyone."

"What I know is that an accident can crush your dreams in a heartbeat. She can't afford to wait around for some doctor's stamp of approval. She'll add time."

"You say that like it's worse than another seizure."

"Sue—" Dad's voice dies off when I step into the kitchen.

"What's on the agenda this morning?" I ask. "Don't tell me. It starts with *s* and ends with *eizure*?"

Mom's leaning against the counter in an oversized T-shirt, nursing a huge cup of coffee. The only sound in the room is the sizzling bacon Dad flips at the stove. Huck, our family's brown Lab, lumbers over to press his face against my thigh.

I run my fingers through the scruff behind his ears. "I mean, if we're having a discussion about my future, I should probably be part of it, right?"

"Let's have breakfast first," Dad says, adding a dripping slice of bacon to the already greasy plate. The stubble on his cheeks is peppered with gray. "We'll think better on full stomachs."

Mom carries her coffee to the table and curls into a chair. Her red hair—thick and wavy like Ali's, instead of flat and strawberry blond like mine—catches the soft morning sunlight through the sliding glass door. "Scrambled or over easy?" Dad asks.

"Scrambled, please."

"Me too," says Mom.

I pour myself a cup of coffee and steal a slice of bacon on my way to the table.

Huck lays his head in my lap, his watery eyes begging me to drop a crumb or two. "So what time are we going to see the doctor?"

"What?" Mom frowns.

"I just need a neurologist to say I'm fine, right? And then I can swim."

"Honey, it doesn't work that way. First of all, their offices won't open until nine or ten. And second of all, it's going to take at least a week or two to get an appointment."

"Two weeks?" Even one missed practice means at least three days in the water to get back on track. "Are you kidding me?"

"Watch your tone," Dad says, using his coaching voice, the one that stops even hulking seniors in their tracks. "Your mother hasn't made the calls yet; somebody can probably squeeze you in."

"And if they can't?"

My parents exchange a look so loaded with tension it's palpable.

"We'll figure something out," says Dad.

"Your safety has to come first," says Mom.

"What about work?" My summer lifeguarding job was supposed to start tomorrow, and a flight to California for Nationals sure isn't free. Plus, there's the cost of a new suit and goggles. My chest tightens. "It's not like Sara's going to hold my spot. She can't be short a guard for two whole weeks."

"I can cover your ticket," says Dad. "But your mom and I agreed it would be better if you worked somewhere else this year."

"Like where? Do you know how hard it is to find a job at this point?"

"Maybe you could find something at the mall?" Dad offers. "If you took an afternoon shift, Mom could drive you, and I'll help when I can."

As the middle-school secretary, Mom's part-time in the summer, and it's true she'll have the flexibility to help with driving. But the idea of spending my summer under the fluorescent lights in the mall, pawning jeggings to over-perfumed tween-agers, while my teammates are lounging around the pool getting tan, feels like salt in an open wound.

"What if I don't have to quit?" I try. "Maybe I could trade my stand shifts for the crappy cleaning jobs until we get this whole thing straightened out."

Dad brings two steaming plates of eggs to the table. "Look, I know this is hard, Tess. If it were up to me, you'd be back in the water already."

Mom takes a big sip of coffee, hiding her expression behind the mug.

"But Mom's definitely right about this," Dad continues, earning a glance of approval. "You can't be responsible for other people's safety until you're officially cleared to swim."

"I'll drive you to the pool tomorrow afternoon so you can talk to Sara in person," Mom says. "I'm sure she'll be disappointed, but we want to let her know as soon as possible so she can find a replacement."

My parents' faces are suddenly twin masks of resolve—my whole summer has already been decided. "On second thought, I'm not that hungry."

On my way out of the kitchen, I scrape my eggs into Huck's bowl and drop my plate in the sink. It clatters against the other dirty dishes with a sound like broken glass.

—

The sharp smell of chlorine welcomes me as I pass through the pool's iron gates. The water gleams in the sunlight, and kids splash and scream with joy.

Sara's kneeling by the baby pool, testing the chlorine. She hurries over, her blue flip-flops slapping against the concrete.

"Tess," she says, the concern on her face barely shadowed by the brim of her baseball cap. "How *are* you?"

I take a protective step backward. I'm fine; I mean, I'm terrible, but that doesn't mean I want to talk about it with my boss.

"Taro told me all about it," she says. "He said that's all people could talk about at practice yesterday."

Taro, Sara's son, is a freshman at Oakwood who cares more about running the team's gossip mill than improving his 100-meter fly. If Taro knows, the whole team knows. Suddenly, I feel like a specimen pinned to a microscope slide.

"Yeah, well, I'm fine. I actually just came to pick up my schedule for the week." I don't know why I say it. All I know is that giving up my job will give Sara something to report back to Taro, and then everyone will know my whole life is falling apart. "I have a doctor's appointment coming up soon. This will all get cleared up then."

"Oh, honey," Sara says. "When I heard what happened, I just assumed..."

"What?"

She lowers her chin. "You know I can't risk the safety of the pool patrons, Tess. I got another application last week. Perfect timing, really. I called him this morning, and he's coming in shortly."

"But I'm fine," I say, horrified by the whine that creeps into my voice.

"Tess, I'm sorry." She's not just apologizing for giving my job away; she's apologizing the way people do after a tragedy, when *I'm sorry* is the only thing they can say to make themselves feel better about someone else's pain.

"It's okay," I lie, staring at the peeling red polish on my toes. Mac painted them last week while we quizzed each other for our Human Anatomy final. "I understand."

"Look," Sara says, "I know it's not much of a consolation, but I could use somebody in the Sugar Shack. The manager got mono, and Taro can't handle it on his own. I could really use the help."

Except for the manager, the snack bar is usually run by junior high kids, who get paid cash to spend a few hours a week slinging ice cream bars and candy to pool patrons. If the pool had a caste system, the snack bar staff would be at the bottom of it.

"Seriously?"

"It'd be good to have someone in there with an actual work

ethic," Sara says. "Last year, we had a run on Swedish Fish that practically caused a riot. I'll even raise the pay—how about twelve bucks an hour?"

It's not my dream job, but I'd still be getting paid. With my dad covering my flight to California, I could easily save up enough for my gear.

"I'll take it."

"Great!" Relief spreads across Sara's face. "Can you start today? I haven't even cleaned up the place."

At this point, anything would be a welcome distraction from the spiraling cesspool that has become my life. "Sure. I just need to let my mom know."

I head to the parking lot, texting Mac on the way.

Mac: **Does it come with benefits? Like free fudge pops?**
Tess: **Doubt it**

She texts a frowny face emoji with a picture of an ice cream cone.

Mom looks up from her phone when I open the van door. "How'd it go?"

I tell her about my conversation with Sara, how the entire team apparently knows about "the incident."

"Well, at least you got a job out of it. That worked out better than expected."

"She wants me to start today."

Mom puts her phone in the cupholder. "Are you sure you're up for that?"

"It's stacking chips, Mom." I glance down at her phone. "Were you stalking Ali again? You already got unfriended on Facebook. You don't want to lose Instagram, too."

"Very funny. I was actually scheduling your neurology appointment. One of the practices I called had a cancellation Thursday and they're squeezing you in."

Relief floods my chest. Six missed practices is bad, but it's not the end of the world. I'll definitely be able to recover in plenty of time for Nationals. "Awesome. I'll let Coach know I'll be back Friday."

"Hold off on that," Mom says. "We need to see what the doctor says before you start planning to get back in the water."

"What are you talking about? The ER doctor said my seizure was probably a one-time thing."

"And she also said we need more testing to know for sure."

"Whose side are you on, Mom?"

"This isn't about sides," Mom says. "Your safety is my only priority."

"Don't you think I'm old enough to decide what's safe for myself?"

"Maybe one day when you have kids, you'll understand."

"When I have kids, I'll support their dreams," I snap, ignoring the nagging guilt that tugs at the back of my mind. Both of my parents have sacrificed to get me where I am.

Mom's jaw tightens. "I'll text you the appointment information," she says, putting on her sunglasses. "You should let Sara know you'll need the day off."

As she pulls out of the lot, I text Mac again:

Tess: Can we hang out later? I really need to talk.
Mac: We're on the way to the pool. See you there?
Tess: Who all is coming?
Mac: Just me and Rachel

Suddenly, I'm wishing I hadn't agreed to work today. It's hard enough that Mac and I spend the summer guarding while the rest of our teammates, whose wealthy parents pay for their gear, work on their tans and take Sunday road trips to the shore. Now that I'm going be doling out candy to toddlers who pay with pennies, I don't know if I'll be able to stand it.

I find Sara inside the Sugar Shack, rummaging in a narrow closet. "I put the ice cream in the freezer already," she says, "but everything else is still in my trunk. The floor needs to be mopped, and it looks like we're going to need a new price sign." She hands me a faded poster board with bent corners. "How long are you here?"

"As long as you need me."

"Perfect." She tosses me her car keys. "The new guard is on his way in, and I still need to get the schedule straightened out for the rest of the month. Can I just leave you to it?"

"Sure."

I head back to the parking lot and hoist three cases of water from Sara's van into my arms.

A yellow Jeep swerves into the empty spot beside me. The speakers are blaring "Margaritaville," a song I only know because of Dad's insistence on listening to the classic rock station whenever he's driving. The guy behind the wheel looks to be my age; he parks the Jeep, cutting off the music.

He's tall and lanky with a shock of black hair above dark sunglasses with thick blue frames, the kind you'd find for a couple of bucks at the 7-11. He's wearing a green T-shirt, loose-fitting jeans, and slides.

"Want some help with that?" he asks, pushing his glasses up into his hair. It sticks out at odd angles, definitely not brushed this morning.

"I'm good," I grunt, pressing my chin into the top case to keep it from slipping.

"Is all of this going inside?"

"Yep."

He grabs a couple things from the trunk and follows me.

Sara greets him as he passes the guard house. "Nice to see you, Charlie," she says. "Looks like you met Tess?"

"Not officially," he says.

I slide the water onto the counter, massaging my lower arm where the corner of the case left a red mark.

"Tess is managing the snack bar this summer," she tells him.

Charlie holds up a box of chips. "Then I guess this belongs to you?"

"Thanks," I mutter.

"Let's talk in the guardhouse." Sara motions for Charlie to follow, but he glances back at me before heading after her.

It doesn't matter that Charlie has a dimple, or that his eyes are the same green as his T-shirt, or that he seems remotely considerate. The only thing I need to know about him is he's going to spend the summer in the job that, two days ago, belonged to me.

I toss the chips onto the counter, nearly overshooting, and head out to the parking lot for another load.

Mac and Rachel stroll into the pool a little while later, both wearing cutoffs slung low over their bikini bottoms. Mac spots me in the snack bar and waves. I stop sweeping and step outside to meet her.

"I missed you at practice." She flings her arms around my neck in an awkward hug. "Coach missed you, too."

"Really?"

"Yeah, you know, in her emotionless robot kind of way." She rifles through the bags on the counter. "Swedish Fish. Good call."

Rachel pads over, a thick towel slung around her neck. "Really moving up in the world, Coop."

My eyes dart to Mackenzie, whose face pales slightly. "I may have mentioned the Sugar Shack gig."

My team would've found out anyway, but it still stings to hear Mac was talking about me behind my back—especially to Rachel.

"C'mon, Mac," Rachel says. "I want a good spot in the sun."

"I'll be there in a minute."

"Doesn't she have her own pool?" I ask as Rachel saunters off. "And, like, servants to torture or something?"

"Apparently she's not allowed to use the pool anymore unless her parents are there."

"Because of what happened?"

"Yeah."

"Great."

Mac sighs. "I know it sucks."

"At least I have a doctor's appointment in a few days. I'll be back in the water soon."

"Already?"

"Well, yeah." Mac's wariness surprises me. She knows how hard it will be to make up a week of missed practice. "With Nationals—"

"Right." Mac changes the subject, her eyes tracking Rachel by the chairs. "So we'll hang out later?"

"Sure." I get back to sweeping, adding angry piles of dust and mouse droppings to the growing heap in the middle of the floor.

—

"Hey." Charlie leans against the snack bar counter. "It's Tess, right? Could I get a Coke? Actually, whatever's cold is fine."

"We're not open for business until tomorrow."

"Sara said I could just grab something on my way out?"

"I didn't realize lifeguards were getting free refreshments this summer."

Charlie drums on the counter, probably wondering why I'm

giving him such a runaround over a fifty-cent soda. To be honest, I'm kind of wondering that, too.

"I think she was just being nice," he says.

I rip open one of the cases of Coke, the cans still hot from Sara's trunk, and slide one across the counter. "Sorry, but there's nothing in the fridge."

Charlie acts like he doesn't even notice it's warm. He just cracks it open and takes a long draw, his Adam's apple bobbing. "Refreshing," he says, lowering his sunglasses. "See you later, Tess."

His arms swing loosely as he walks away, like he doesn't have a care in the world.

CHAPTER
FOUR

It's five when my alarm jerks me from a restless sleep. It's still dark outside, and for a second, I consider hitting snooze. It's not like I can go to practice anyway. But that kind of thinking will slow me down. If I can't train in the pool, I can at least go for a run.

Dad's in the kitchen, waiting for the coffee to finish brewing. He wears an undershirt and pajama bottoms, his brown hair flat in the front and sleep lines crisscrossing his face. "Morning," he says. "Why are you up so early?"

"Going for a run." I grab a banana from the fruit basket. "Better than nothing, right?" Dad and I both know it's impossible to make up a practice on dry land, especially since I'm a full day behind the rest of the team. But some workout is definitely better than no workout.

"Want me to get the weights out of the basement?" Dad asks.

"Sure." I pop a chunk of banana in my mouth. "I'll look up one of Coach's workouts to do on my own."

"That's my girl." The coffee pot chirps, and Dad reaches for a mug. "Have a cup with me first?"

"No thanks. The win doesn't wait, remember?"

A sleepy smile crinkles the skin at the corners of Dad's eyes. Those words, announced many mornings in my predawn bedroom when I was younger, motivated me to get up for the two-hour practice I'd have before school. "I knew you wouldn't let this hold you back."

Pride flickers, its soft glow spreading warmth throughout my chest. Dad's always been my biggest fan. No matter what happens at my doctor's appointment, I know he'll find a way to get me back in the water.

"Maybe I should start lifting again," Dad muses.

"Might help with the whole high-cholesterol thing."

"Shush! You'll give your mom ideas!"

Huck and I head outside into the dusky morning where, even at this hour, humidity has settled over the neighborhood like a damp blanket. Dew drips from the leaves of daylilies that yawn open in Mom's carefully tended flower bed.

I cue up my race playlist, adjust my earbuds, and mentally map out a decent five-mile route with a few good hills. Soon I'm sweating from the heat, but my muscles relish the movement. The repetitive pounding of my feet against the pavement, the steady inhale and exhale of my breath, and the throbbing beat of the music lulls my brain into quiet complacency.

My neighborhood is mostly still asleep, but just ahead, a ratty dog squats to pee in front of a brick house. I lead Huck to the other side of the road, scanning for the dog's owner. She's leaning against the open side door in a tank top and pajama bottoms, an oversized mug clutched in her hands.

She spots us at the same time the dog does. Its ears perk up and it growls.

"No, Pickles," she warns in a voice that cracks with sleep. "Come!"

It's no use. The deranged little rodent charges across the street right at us.

I pull Huck's leash, hoping if we keep moving, the other dog won't follow, but Huck just freezes like a possum.

"Shit, shit, shit," the woman mutters, hurrying barefoot down the driveway, one arm wrapped across her bouncing, clearly bra-less chest and the other still clutching the giant mug. "Get over here!"

"Come on, Huck!" I tug at his leash, but he just stands there yelping while the smaller dog snarls and circles his feet, nipping at his ankles.

"Stop that!" The woman awkwardly tries to scoop up Pickles while also keeping her mug upright. She finally gets a hand on the wiry scruff of the dog's neck, but he quickly wriggles out of her grasp.

I'm so focused on getting Huck out of this situation and getting back to my run, that I don't hear the footsteps approaching until they're right behind me. I jerk around, surprised to see Charlie in a T-shirt and running shorts.

"Hey there, Pickles," he says, squatting down to pick up the little monster. The dog squirms for a minute, its legs swimming in the air, but it quickly nuzzles against Charlie's chest and licks the bottom of his chin. "That's a good boy." Charlie hands the dog over to the clearly frazzled woman.

An exhausted exhale puffs her cheeks out like a balloon. Fine dark hairs stick to the sweat that shines on her forehead. She uses her free arm to press the now-relaxed mutt against her chest. "Sorry about that. I thought he'd just pee and come right back in."

"It's no problem," I say, forcing a neighborly smile. Huck, my vicious guard dog, collapses on the asphalt, panting. Charlie stoops to scratch him behind the ear and Huck's tongue lolls out of his mouth.

"You coming in for breakfast?" the woman asks Charlie.

"Sure." He lifts the collar of his shirt to wipe the sweat off his upper lip. "Right behind you."

Pickles wriggles against the woman's chest and yaps, apparently remembering Huck's presence. "See you inside," she says to Charlie, and then as an afterthought, "Sorry again."

"You live here?" I ask Charlie. "I've never seen you around before."

"Do you know all your neighbors?" His brow quirks in a way that makes my cheeks feel hot, and not from the exercise.

"No," I say, louder than I mean to.

"It's my aunt's place," Charlie says. "We're just crashing for a while."

I vaguely remember seeing a U-Haul pass by my house during the last week of school. Our neighborhood is full of what Dad calls "starter homes," even though we've lived in ours my whole life. People are always moving in and out.

"Do you want to come in?" Charlie asks. "Denise makes a mean Pop-Tart."

The offer takes me off guard. "Seriously?"

"I mean, we're going to be working together all summer. Don't you think we should get to know each other?"

"We do *not* work together," I correct him. "You're a lifeguard, and I'm in the Sugar Shack. Big difference."

"So does that mean there's some weird social hierarchy at the pool? Because if there is, you should probably just explain it to me. I've never really been good at that stuff."

"Look, I just want to finish my run, okay?"

Charlie gives me a half smile, the shadow of a dimple flashing across his cheek. "Sure. See you around, neighbor."

I put in my earbuds and break into a jog, Huck panting heavily behind me.

"But he's so hot!" Mac sits on the snack bar counter after her shift, her bare feet swinging back and forth. Behind her, a dwindling line of kids waits for candy and ice cream bars. "Even for a narp." Most of my teammates prefer to date swimmers, avoiding "non-athletic regular people" who can't understand the level of commitment we have to our sport. "Yeah, well, he's also a weirdo," I say. "Who invites a complete stranger in for breakfast?"

A little girl slides a dollar across the counter and whispers that she would like a hundred Swedish Fish. A penny a fish was a terrible idea.

Mac twists around to look out at the pool. Two days into summer and her olive skin is already a glowing golden brown. "A little quirkiness never hurt anybody. I like it when a guy's not afraid to be himself."

I drop the fish five at a time into a cup and follow Mac's gaze to the lifeguard stand, where Charlie perches in all his sun-god glory. His tan skin is beaded with sweat, accentuating lean muscles. A couple tweeny-boppers pass his chair, giggling—I swear, you can practically see cartoon hearts popping out of their eyes. Even a few moms ogle him as they lounge on the chairs, pretending to watch their kids.

"Then you must really like Charlie."

A mischievous smile plays at the corners of Mac's mouth. "I think somebody has a little crush."

"I do not! Just because everybody else around here is going gaga over him, doesn't mean I am."

Mac cocks her brow, and even the little girl waiting for candy looks doubtful.

"I don't have a crush on him!" I shout, ducking my head as a few of the other kids in line peer at me curiously.

"Besides," I say, lowering my voice, "after my doctor's appointment tomorrow, I'll be back in the water, and I have some serious catching up to do before Nationals. I don't have time for boys."

Mac rolls her eyes. "Then let's definitely hang out this weekend—you know, before you go all turbo with training."

"What'd you have in mind?"

She sneaks a fallen fish. "Seth's having a party. Nothing big, just the team. You should come."

"I don't know," I say. "I definitely want to hang out, but I was thinking more along the lines of Froyo and *Friends*."

Mac groans.

"Um, excuse me," the little girl says, her fingers gripping the edge of the counter. Her face is streaked with white sunscreen, and her brown eyes are wide and watery. "That was only ninety-two. I counted."

The cup is filled almost to the brim with Swedish Fish. I drop an uncounted handful on the top. "Happy?"

Her eyes light up as she slides her candy off the counter. Another kid waves a dollar in my face. "Can I have a fudge pop, please?"

It's going to be a very long summer.

"Look, I get that parties aren't really your thing," Mac presses, "but it wouldn't kill you to loosen up a little. So far, this summer has sucked, and you deserve to have some fun. We both do."

She's right about that. I have zero interest in hanging out with Rachel and her friends, but a fun night out could be the reset this summer needs.

"I'll think about it."

Mac squeals. "I'll take that as a yes."

Rachel strolls over, a baggy T-shirt hanging off one shoulder. She lowers her oversized sunglasses. "Uh, Mac, aren't we heading out soon? It's almost two."

"Shoot!" Mac hops down, her damp bathing suit leaving a wet smudge across the counter. "I'll call you tonight, okay?"

"Actually, I was kind of wondering if I could get a ride home? My mom isn't off until four."

"What time does your shift end?"

"In an hour."

Mac glances at Rachel.

"Mac and I made plans to go to the mall before practice," Rachel says.

"I guess we could wait?" Mac's offer sounds like a question, like maybe she's hoping I won't say yes. The air between us feels taut, like a rubber band stretched too tight.

Rachel frowns. "Seriously?"

"It's fine." I pretend Mac doesn't look relieved. "I can just wait here for my mom."

"Are you sure?" she asks.

Here's what I want to say: *No, I'm not sure. Ditch the bitch and hang out here with me.*

Here's what I say: "Yeah. You guys go ahead."

"Six months will pass before you know it," Mac says.

"Sure." I take a dollar from the next kid in line and shove it into the cashbox. "It's going to fly by." My soon-to-be confiscated license is burning a hole in my wallet. I don't even know why I'm carrying it around.

Mac blows me a kiss over her shoulder as she trails after Rachel.

I toss the kid his Drumstick and grab my phone to text my mom.

Tess: **Can you pick me up after work?**

Mom: **Can't Mac bring you home?**

If I tell her Mac's under the spell of a devious best-friend-stealing witch, she'll want to talk about it, and the last thing I need is my mom scrutinizing another aspect of my life.

Tess: **She couldn't make it to the pool today. Come get me pls?**

Like a freshman, completely reliant on my mom for rides, I wait anxiously for her response.

A thumbs-up emoji pops onto my screen.

Mom: **Be there by 4:15.**

I take the next kid's order, consoling myself with the reminder I'll be back in the water by Friday. Maybe the doctor will even say I can drive.

As Mac and Rachel leave, an unfamiliar feeling sprouts in my gut, green and bitter. I take a swig of water, washing the feeling away.

—

The red Nissan Sentra parked in Mom's usual spot in the driveway has a missing hubcap and a conspicuous dent where the car once caught the fire hydrant at the end of our street.

Ali's home.

Mom and I exchange glances as she parks the van next to the Nissan. "Did you know she was coming today?"

"Didn't you?"

In the living room, Ali's lounging on the couch, her toes tucked under a sleeping Huck as she nurses a Venti coffee. She's dressed in a tank top and yoga pants, her red hair in a messy topknot.

"Surprise!" She stands, nudging Huck off the couch.

Mom wraps her in a hug. "You should've told us you were coming. I would've come home early."

"It was sort of spur of the moment," Ali explains. She tugs at my tank top, stiff with sweat from a day in the unairconditioned Sugar Shack. "When was the last time you showered?"

"Missed you, too," I grumble.

"What sounds good for dinner?" Mom asks. "Dad will be home any minute, and I'm sure you're hungry after the drive from the city."

"Starved," Ali says.

In the kitchen, Mom ties an apron over her work clothes while Ali searches the pantry, settling on a fresh bag of potato chips. Salt and vinegar—my favorite.

Mom frowns. "Maybe the three of us could have some girl time after Tess's appointment tomorrow? I took the whole day off. We could go out for lunch, get our nails done?"

"Sounds fun," Ali says, settling onto a stool at the kitchen island. "But don't make any special plans because of me. I'm staying awhile."

"What's 'awhile'?" I ask, thinking about the single upstairs bathroom I already share with Mom and Dad.

Ali shrugs. "At least the summer." She pops a chip in her mouth, the crunching audible in the otherwise silent kitchen.

"The whole summer?" I exclaim. My sister is a messy, highly opinionated night owl, best enjoyed in small doses.

"I thought you'd be happy," she says. "When was the last time you and I got to spend any time together?"

Mom's voice is high and tight in her throat. "You know you're welcome anytime, honey, but—"

"I'm between gigs. Dad said driving was an issue, so—"

"You talked to your dad about this?"

"I mean, I didn't tell him I decided to come, but yeah. We talk a lot actually."

Mom's lips press together.

"You're looking at your new Uber driver." Ali winks at me. "Tips are much appreciated."

"Mom—"

"It's very thoughtful of you," Mom says firmly, "but don't you think it's a little rash? You don't need to uproot your life for us. We're doing fine."

"Fine," I echo, rescuing my chips before they disappear.

"It's really no big deal." Ali brushes crumbs off her hands. "I can waitress anywhere."

"But your apartment—"

"Already found a subletter. Honestly, Mom, this is a no-brainer for me."

"We'll talk more when your dad's home, okay?" Mom carries a pot to the sink, turns on the water. "I'll make spaghetti."

Ali gestures for me to sit beside her. "Come fill me in," she says. "Any juicy gossip I should know about?"

"Not really," I say. "I mean, there is this party Saturday."

"Ooh, fun!" Ali's whole body perks up. "Who's going to be there?"

"Just the team. I can go, right, Mom?"

"Please tell me I can help pick out your outfit," Ali says.

"I don't know," Mom says. "I don't love the idea of you being out late right now."

"It's not like I'll be alone."

"C'mon, Mom," Ali urges. "She'll be fine. Fun is exactly what she needs right now."

Mom puts the pot on the stove. "Fine. But home by midnight, okay?"

"Sure," I say, shocked at how easily Mom caved. *Thank you*, I mouth to Ali.

She snatches back the chips. "What are big sisters for?"

CHAPTER
FIVE

The waiting room in the neurologist's office is freezing, and goose-bumps prickle the skin on my bare legs. The room smells like industrial air freshener, the kind that squirts from the ceiling in a public bathroom. A little boy with a helmet plays with the bin of LEGOs while his dad flips through a magazine. A girl who looks younger than me scans her phone, and the woman next to her jostles a fussy toddler, plying him with gummy bears. I wonder which one of them is here to see the doctor.

"Stop bouncing," Mom says, putting a flat palm on my knee. "You're making me nervous." Her lipstick, hastily applied in the rearview mirror before we came inside, smudges a little under her lower lip.

I curl my sneakers around the legs of my chair and sit on my hands. A nurse in pale blue scrubs steps into the waiting room and invites me and Mom back.

After checking my weight and blood pressure, the nurse escorts us to an exam room with bare blue walls and a bleach-white floor. A petite woman enters and introduces herself as Dr. Cappalano.

She settles onto the swivel stool, opens her laptop, and skims what I assume are my records. "So you had a seizure," she says.

"Apparently," I say lightly, which is the opposite of how I feel.

Dr. Cappalano's eyes flicker across the screen. "I see the hospital EEG was inconclusive."

Mom has her notebook out, and she gives the doctor the details of my night in the ER. Dr. Cappalano's fingers fly across the keyboard. Then she turns to me. "What do you remember about that night?"

"Not much. One minute I was swimming, and the next, I wasn't." I don't tell her what it felt like to wake up on the concrete, wet and shivering, blinking at the blurry face of the EMT. I don't tell her what it felt like to hear my friends crying.

"What about the week before?" she asks. "Were you overly stressed, dehydrated, or sleep-deprived?"

"You're pretty much describing Tess's natural state," Mom says.

Dr. Cappalano arches her brow.

"I'm a competitive swimmer," I explain. "It's kind of a high-pressure lifestyle."

Mom sniffs, and I cut my eyes at her. "I think I manage it pretty well."

The room is silent, except for the clicking keyboard. My stomach growls, and I wish I'd eaten more than a granola bar for breakfast.

The doctor stands and squirts sanitizer into her palm. "I just need to do a neurological exam, and then we'll get you on your way." She holds up one finger and asks me to follow it with my eyes as she moves it to the left and then to the right. That's the first in a series of requests that seem similar to the things cops on TV do when they pull over drunk drivers. *Touch your finger to your nose. Walk heel to toe in a straight line.* I do everything she asks with ease.

"Great," Dr. Cappalano says when we're finished. "Perfectly normal."

I flash Mom a smile, but her eyes are still glued to the doctor.

"It's not uncommon to see isolated seizures in people who don't have epilepsy," Dr. Cappalano says, confirming what we already know. "A very stressful time or extreme sleep deprivation can sometimes provoke a one-time seizure."

"So what happened to me *was* a fluke?" I press.

"Well, what you're describing about your life makes me think you have a pretty high tolerance for that kind of stress. And then there's the inconclusive EEG..." She taps her nails against the back of her laptop, like she's formulating a plan.

"I thought you just said this was a one-time thing."

"She said it could have been," Mom says softly.

"I think we should do further testing," Dr. Cappalano says. "I'd like to start with an extended EEG—an hour. Depending on what that shows us, I may suggest a twenty-four-hour ambulatory EEG."

After my hospital EEG, it had taken several washes to remove the sticky remnants of glue that held the electrodes in place on my scalp. "Twenty-four hours?" I ask.

"It's overnight, but you'd wear the testing device home."

"How long is this all going to take?"

"They'll schedule the EEG at the front desk for you. You can probably get in next week."

Next week? I need to get back in the water now. "Can't we skip all that?" I ask. "Just give me meds or something. I'll do whatever you want."

Dr. Cappalano folds her hands in her lap. "I know this is hard. But we can't just medicate you until we know what's going on with your body. And we just don't know until we know."

"You mean until I have another seizure?"

Mom releases an audible exhale.

"Unfortunately, yes." The doctor turns back to her laptop. "They'll have the paperwork ready for you at checkout." She stands up and shakes my hand. "You can expect to hear from me once the results come in."

"What about swimming?" I blurt.

"My preference would be for you to avoid it until we get a clear idea of what we're up against here. If you lost consciousness in the water..."

The solid table beneath me seems to give way, and I grasp for an edge of certainty.

"What if I did it anyway?"

The doctor's eyes search my face. "I want to be clear: swimming could be dangerous. But if you're going to do it anyway, there are safety measures you could take to reduce the risk of a serious seizure injury."

Hope whispers through my chest. Mom reopens her notebook, her pen poised over the page.

"You'll need to wear a brightly colored swim cap," Dr. Cappalano begins. As she continues listing safety precautions—including swimming in the outer lane, usually reserved for the slowest swimmers—I realize the things on this list won't keep me from having a seizure. They'll just make it easier for my coach and teammates to fish me out of the water if I do.

Red and blue emergency lights flash, and the air is cold against my wet skin. *You were so stiff*, Mac had said. *We could barely keep your face above water.*

I press my hands against the exam table, grounding myself in the present. My seizure was a one-time thing. These precautions are just in case, until the EEG results confirm what I already know: everything's fine, and in a few short months, this will all be an unpleasant memory.

"One more thing," Dr. Cappalano says. "Your body is still recovering, so you'll need to be careful not to overdo it. Take it easy, okay?"

This close to Nationals, there's no such thing as taking it easy. Swimming through illness, injury, and sheer exhaustion is the name of the game. Because while my entry time means I'm expected to swim in the A Finals, grouped with the fastest swimmers at the event, the results of a preliminary race each morning determine which swimmers I'll race against at night. If I don't make my time at preliminaries, I could end up in the B Finals, or worse, the Cs—not what the Northern Hills coach will want to see from me the summer before I sign to swim with his team. I have every intention of securing my spot in the A Finals, no matter how hard I have to train. So if Dr. Cappalano's going to let me swim, I'll tell her anything she wants to hear. "This is temporary, right? Just a precaution?"

"Hopefully," the doctor says. "We'll know more once we get back the EEG results."

She shakes our hands again before leaving the room. Mom and I sit quietly for a minute, listening as the doctor's short, square heels retreat down the hall.

"At least I can get back in the water."

"She said it could be dangerous," Mom says.

"Which is why I'd be taking precautions."

Mom's eyes drop to the page of scribbled training modifications in her notebook. "I just don't think we need to rush things. It's only another week."

"She said I can swim, Mom. I'm going to swim."

Mom drops her notebook into her purse. "Then you should probably set up a meeting with Coach Higgins. We'll need to make sure she's on board with all of this."

While I'm pretty sure Coach will be fine with the doctor's restrictions, wearing a neon cap and swimming in the outside lane will announce one more way I'm different than my teammates. How can something I've done my whole life suddenly be dangerous?

"Want to grab Ali for lunch at Paprika?" Mom asks.

"Sure." I hoist myself off the table and pluck torn pieces of paper from the backs of my legs. Everything's going to be fine. This is temporary, right? Just temporary.

———

Cars sprinkle the lot at Oakwood Academy where evening practice has just ended. Dad parks the van, and Mom twists around in her seat. "Are you sure you want to do this?"

"Of course I do," I tell her.

"Of course she does," Dad says.

"I just don't understand the harm in waiting until we get the EEG results," Mom says for the hundredth time since my doctor's appointment.

"We've had this conversation, Sue." Dad opens his door, letting in a rush of warm air. "If Oakwood won't accommodate the safety requirements, she's not swimming. But we won't know unless we ask."

"Coach is waiting," I plead.

Mom sighs, steeling herself. Then she reaches for her purse.

Together, we enter the school and head down the long hallway toward Coach's cramped office. She stands when she sees us, comes around her desk, and waves us in.

"How are you feeling?" she asks, gripping my shoulders. Her

blond hair is swept into a tight ponytail under her signature visor, and her slate-gray eyes scan my body like she's looking for signs of damage.

"I'm good," I say. "Ready to train."

Coach looks at my parents, who hover just inside the door. "Have a seat," she says, gesturing to the narrow chairs opposite her desk. "I assume your doctor approved this?"

The same uncertainty Mom has worn since my appointment hangs from her shoulders like an old coat, heavy and uncomfortable. She opens her mouth, but I jump in first: "We saw the doctor yesterday, and she said I can swim as I long as I take a few temporary precautions."

Coach folds her hands behind her head and leans back in her chair as she listens to Dr. Cappalano's instructions.

She's quiet when I've finished. Her chair creaks as she sits upright.

"We know this is a lot," Mom says a bit too eagerly. "And we understand if you're uncomfortable."

"We can work with—" Dad starts, but Coach interrupts him.

"You'd take the outside lane?"

"Yes," I say.

"And a neon cap."

"Absolutely."

"Davis will have to stay by your lane the whole time."

Nobody said anything about being babysat by the assistant coach, but at this point, I'll agree to anything if it gets me back in the water. "Please, Coach."

She tents her hands under her chin, considering. "I'll have to run this by administration, but I don't foresee any issues. Unless we hear otherwise in the next couple days, you can plan to come back to practice Monday."

The rush of relief is sudden and intense; I grip the back of Dad's chair. "Thank you, Coach. Thank you so much!"

Mom's smile is strained, and I know she was silently hoping that Coach would deny our request.

Dad pumps Coach's hand. "You won't regret this."

"I'm happy to make this work. Your daughter's an excellent swimmer with a bright future ahead. But, Tess," she says, "with modified training this late in the year, we may need to be realistic about our expectations for Nationals."

I nod, trying to look as serious as I possibly can when my insides are exploding with joy. My EEG is next Wednesday. I only have to get through a week with these modifications, and then I'm off the hook. The fastest you'll ever see a fish swim is when it finally realizes it's free.

CHAPTER
SIX

"Ladies," Seth greets me and Mac as we weave through his crowded kitchen. So much for a small party. The whole team is here, along with half the school. "You two are looking hot tonight!" Seth slides his arm around Mac's waist, pulling her in for a quick kiss on the cheek.

Mac beams. She does look gorgeous, her curly hair dried into loose waves, her white shorts and peach crop top showing off her deep tan. Next to her, I feel like an overdressed mannequin. The sundress Ali made me wear feels too short, my wedges too high.

Seth fills two cups with pink liquid from a crystal punch bowl. Soggy maraschino cherries and pineapple chunks sink to the bottom.

"Jungle Juice," he says, handing us the drinks. "My secret recipe."

Mac toasts my cup with hers. "To summer."

"To summer!" Seth tosses back a shot of something syrupy and brown.

"To summer and its new beginning," I say, taking a hesitant sip. Mac cheers.

Turns out Jungle Juice tastes like a mixture of Kool-Aid and nail polish remover. Mac's face pinches as she swallows, but she licks her lips and flashes Seth a smile. "Yummy!"

"Omigod, Mac!" Rachel shrieks. She rushes across the room, hands flapping like a crazed chicken, and flings her arms around Mac's neck. Jungle Juice sloshes on the floor.

Rachel wears a floral tube top and a denim miniskirt, and her flushed cheeks sparkle with glittery powder. When Mac hugs her, jealousy slithers around my stomach and squeezes.

"I need a partner for beer pong," Rachel says. "You in?"

"Sure!" Mac casts me a guilty look, like she just remembered I'm here.

Rachel cuts her eyes at me. "I've never seen you in heels before."

I tug down the hem of my dress. "Beer pong?" I ask Mac. "You have to drive, remember?"

"One drink, two tops. Want to come?"

I shake my head, and Rachel tugs on Mac's arm. "I'll be right back," Mac says.

Rachel pulls her toward the dining room, and an uneasy feeling settles over me. In this room that's packed with people, I suddenly feel completely alone.

I tolerate the party for as long as I can, but everybody wants to know the gory details of my seizure. How it felt, whether I'm scared of having another one, and how grateful I must be to Mac and Rachel for saving my life. Nearly ready to bail, I head outside for some fresh air. There's a keg in Seth's backyard with a small crowd hovering near it. Others lounge around a glowing firepit.

I slip my shoes off and pick my way across the grass, my feet relishing the freedom. A cool nighttime breeze ruffles my dress against my thighs, making me wish I'd brought Ali's leather jacket after all.

Someone's roasting marshmallows—the smell tickles my nose. As I get closer, I realize it's not just someone: it's Charlie.

I drop my shoes and sit down, eyeing the s'mores supplies. "You would raid the kitchen, wouldn't you?"

"It's not a campfire without s'mores." He perches on the edge of his chair, toasting two marshmallows over the flames.

"This is an Oakwood party."

"How do you know I don't go to Oakwood?"

Charlie's faded vintage T-shirt and the worn patch on his jeans don't exactly scream college preparatory. "Let's just say you don't really look the part."

"And you do, I guess?"

I fold my arms across my borrowed sundress.

"A girl from the pool invited me. She lost interest when I wasn't down for beer pong."

I give him a curious glance. "You're not drinking?"

"Nah."

"Why not?"

"Do I have to have a reason?" He glances at my cup. "Why are you drinking?"

I set my barely touched Jungle Juice in the grass by my feet. "I'm not really. Pretty sure I could clean my bathroom with this."

Charlie chuckles, pulling the marshmallows out of the fire and sliding them onto a graham cracker with chocolate. "S'more?"

"Thanks."

He spears two more marshmallows. "So, since you do go to Oakwood, why are you hiding out here?"

"Parties aren't really my scene," I say. "Plus, I'm pretty sure I'd have to put my shoes back on."

"I'm more of a firepit guy myself." He glances at my half-eaten s'more. "Want another one?"

Three s'mores in, and we've already covered favorite movies (rom-coms for me; Charlie likes sci-fi), breakfast food (we're both hardcore pancake fans), and have now moved on to sports.

"You really practice every day?" Charlie asks, toasting his fourth marshmallow.

"Twice a day, actually. Except Sunday. But it's worth it. Our team is headed to Nationals in August."

"So that means I'm sharing my s'mores with one of the best swimmers in the country?"

I smirk. "Pretty much."

"Wow. Will I be able to watch you on TV and throw popcorn at the other swimmers?"

"Yep." My stomach squirms at the thought of Charlie watching me swim. Which is weird because anybody can watch online if they really want to. "What about you? How often do you run?"

"Whenever I feel like it. Why, do you want to come?"

"Nope. I run alone. It's peaceful." I shoot him a look. "Usually."

"In case you've forgotten, I rescued you."

"It was a dog, not a dragon. And I don't need rescuing. I can take care of myself."

"Why does that not surprise me?"

My cheeks suddenly feel hot, and I stare at the fire to avoid looking at Charlie.

"I'm not really into organized sports," he says.

"Too bad. I was beginning to think we had something in common."

"Aw, c'mon. Even with the whole pancake thing?"

I grin. "Waffles really are overrated."

"Totally."

"Too filling."

"And they take too long to make."

"And those annoying little squares."

Charlie laughs out loud, and I like the sound. I want to make him laugh again.

"Let's go get some," he says. "Pancakes, I mean. Definitely not waffles."

"What, like, now?"

"Sure. Why not?"

"Lots of reasons." I glance down at my phone. "One, I have to be home at midnight. Two, I came with my best friend, and I can't just leave her here. Girl code and all that. And three, I don't really know you. As far as I can tell, you're just some guy with a rabid dog and a serious sugar problem."

Charlie pops a perfectly toasted marshmallow into his mouth. "Spontaneity isn't really your thing, is it?"

Now he sounds like Mac. "I can totally be spontaneous. I just spontaneously ate three s'mores, didn't I?" I leave out the part about how I'm going to run six miles to burn off the extra calories before Monday's practice.

"Wow. You're a real wild child." Charlie waves his finger around in the world's most miniature celebration.

"You know what?" I stand, tugging down the back of my dress. "You want to go to breakfast? Let's go to breakfast." I check the time again. "We have exactly forty-two minutes, so you better hurry up."

"Seriously? You're not going to turn into a pumpkin or something?"

"No, but I do have to go tell Mac."

"I can wait," Charlie says, gathering up the s'mores supplies.

I find Mac tucked under Seth's arm in the living room, her mascara smudged, a half-empty beer in her hand. "It's time to go," I tell her.

"What? No! It's not even midnight!" Her words smoosh into each other like Charlie's marshmallows.

"I have to be home by midnight, remember?" My parents had not budged on that point, no matter how hard Ali had pushed for a later curfew on my behalf. "Plus, you're my ride." Though by the looks of it, driving is the last thing Mac should be doing.

Seth pulls her closer. "I'll get her home."

Mac's face lights up.

"No way," I say. "My sister will come get us."

It takes both hands to get Mac to her feet. I lift her arm over my shoulder and steer her out to the front porch. Sinking onto the top step, she drops her chin onto her palm, eyelids heavy.

Tess: **Mac's wasted. Come get us?**

Ali doesn't respond to my text, and my call is sent straight to voicemail.

Tess: **Hello?!!!**

Nothing.

Mac's fallen asleep, her head lolling forward onto her chest. I could drive, but the risk of getting pulled over with an inactive license is way too high. And if I call my parents, I can kiss any remnant of freedom goodbye. There's only one person at this party I know hasn't been drinking. Charlie's going to have to drive us home.

I leave Mac on the steps and head back to the firepit. "Change of plans," I tell Charlie.

"Let me guess," he says. "You are going to turn into a pumpkin?"

"Very funny. I actually need a favor. Mac's wasted. Could you give us a ride home? It's on the way. I know it's not pancakes, but—"

"Sure," Charlie says, surprising me with his willingness. "Let's go."

We find Mac curled up on her side. Somebody literally steps over her on their way down the stairs.

"She's gonna feel great in the morning," Charlie says.

I lift Mac's arm around my shoulder, but when I try to stand, she barely budges. Charlie helps me get her on her feet.

"Can't we stay a little longer?" she moans.

"I think you're all partied out," Charlie says as we make our way to his Jeep.

Mac groans as I buckle her in. "I don't feel so good."

"If she barfs in my baby, I'm never sharing s'mores with you again," Charlie says.

"She won't," I promise.

We've only made it one street over before Mac lurches forward, clutching her stomach. "I'm going to be sick!"

"Pull over!" I shout, but Charlie's already swerving toward the curb. He leans over Mac and pushes the passenger door open as pink vomit splatters to the ground. Breathing through my mouth, I gather her hair back from her face, waiting for the second round.

"Jungle Juice doesn't smell any better the second time around," Charlie sniffs.

We have to stop two more times before we finally reach Mac's neighborhood, a few streets down from our own.

"Need help?" Charlie asks as I open Mac's door.

After clearing her system, Mac is better able to support her own weight. "I've got her," I tell him. "It might be a minute, okay?"

"I'm not going anywhere." He lowers his seat and folds his arms behind his head.

No one's in the living room; the house is dark and quiet. I push

Mac up the stairs, but a creaking door sends my heart into my throat. Mrs. Braverman appears at the top of the staircase.

"Tess? Are you sleeping over tonight?"

"I'm just picking up something I left here," I try.

"At this time of night?" Mrs. Braverman's face contorts as the smell of vomit meets her nose. "Have you girls been drinking?"

That's when I notice the pink chunks in Mac's hair. We're screwed.

Mrs. Braverman hurries down the stairs and lifts her daughter's arm over her shoulder. "After everything your mother's been through," she says.

"I wasn't drinking, Mrs. Braverman, I swear."

"Mom…" Mac moans.

"Don't even try it, Mackenzie." Mrs. Braverman points an angry finger at me. "I'm calling your parents to pick you up."

"My sister's right outside. I promise I'll get home safely."

Mrs. Braverman leans in to sniff my breath. "I believe you, but it would be irresponsible not to let your parents know about this. I'm taking Mackenzie to bed. When I get back, we'll talk about…"

"Mom!" Mac cries. "I'm gonna puke!"

Mrs. Braverman rushes Mac up the stairs, and I take the opportunity to escape.

Charlie sits up when I open the Jeep door. "That was quick."

"Hurry up," I say. "We have to get out of here."

"Hang on. I didn't agree to aiding and abetting…"

"Just go!"

Charlie cranks the Jeep and pulls away from the curb. He's being an annoyingly careful driver, barely going the speed limit. Any minute now Mrs. Braverman is going to call my mom and I'll have hell to pay. My foot guns an invisible gas pedal. "Can't this thing go any faster?"

"*Can* and *will* are two very different things. I am not getting pulled over in a car that smells like puke. Ever heard of a breathalyzer?"

"You weren't drinking."

"Yeah, but you were."

"I highly doubt two sips of Jungle Juice would show up on a breathalyzer."

Charlie gives me a sideways glance. "Then why didn't you drive Mac home yourself?"

"Trust me, if I could've, I would've."

"You don't drive?"

"More like can't. Temporarily anyway."

"Why?"

If Charlie really hasn't heard about my seizure, he's the only person in town who hasn't. Or maybe he's just the only person who hasn't asked about it.

"I had a seizure," I admit. "I can't drive for six months."

"Oh." Charlie's quiet for a minute. "Is that why you can't life-guard this summer?"

"Yep." I fold my arms across my chest. I've given Charlie a window to peek through, and I wait for him to start examining my life through the glass. But unlike the people at the party, Charlie doesn't ask what a seizure feels like. He doesn't tell me how grateful I must be to Mac for saving my life.

"That really sucks," he says.

I stare at the side of his face, the slope of his nose, the sharp angle of his jaw.

He turns on the music, and James Taylor croons softly into the night. Charlie doesn't ask questions. We don't talk anymore at all.

—

Huck barks when I open the door. "Hush," I tell him. "It's just me."

Mom's watching TV in the living room; Dad's dozing in the leather recliner, but he jerks awake. "What'd I miss?"

"It's Tess," Mom tells him. "She just got home." She mutes the cop show she's watching. It's from a hundred years ago, the images all grainy and blue. "Mrs. Braverman called."

Shit.

Huck sniffs the air approvingly and lumbers back to bed.

"Look, Mom..."

"She said you girls had been drinking."

Dad rubs his glossy eyes. "You're in training."

"Not to mention your scholarship," Mom adds. "You know we could never afford Oakwood without it. And you risk it on one stupid night? Your whole future could blow up like"—Mom snaps—"that!"

"I wasn't drinking," I protest, "but it's not like I could drive myself home."

The blue glow of the TV glints off Mom's glasses. "That's another thing: How *did* you get home? Mrs. Braverman said Ali drove you, but I know that was a lie. She's been upstairs all night."

Yeah, not answering her phone. If she had just responded to one of my texts, I might not be in this situation right now. "Someone I know from the pool drove us. And I promise, he wasn't drinking either."

Mom and Dad exchange glances. Their silent communication isn't hard to read—they're trying to decide whether or not I'm in trouble.

"Why didn't you call us?" Dad asks. "You know the deal. If you ever need to get out of a situation, you call and we'll come get you. No questions asked." This has been our family rule ever since Ali got her license, but while she used it a few times, I've never had a reason to.

"I couldn't leave Mac alone."

"We would've driven her, too," Mom argues.

"Yeah, and then you would've called her parents. Just like Mrs. Braverman did."

"Honey, sometimes safety is more important than whether or not you get in trouble. You, above all people, should know that."

Another reference to my seizure. I can't even get in trouble without the shadow of that experience darkening the situation, making everything worse. All I wanted was one night to put it behind me and start the summer fresh. Turns out even that was a risk I can't afford.

"Look, Tess," Dad says. "We trust you. But sneaking around, lying—don't give us a reason not to, okay?"

"I won't," I promise before heading upstairs. There are way more important things on the line this summer than parties and boys. I broke all my own rules tonight, but I won't let it happen again.

Ali's bedroom door is open. Whistling snores rise from her sleeping form, tempting me to shake her awake. My sister has always been a flake, but just when I thought I could actually count on her, she bails. I should've known better.

In my room, I kick off my sandals and climb into bed. My hair smells like campfire, and my teeth are coated with fuzzy sugar sweaters. I send a quick text to Mac:

Tess: **You okay?**

She doesn't respond.

I pull the comforter up to my chin and stare at the ceiling—the sticky remnants of glow-in-the-dark stars that long ago stopped shining. Ever since my seizure, I've been waiting for things to go back to normal, but the only time I felt normal tonight was when I was hanging out with Charlie. He's messy, unmotivated, and clearly doesn't care what people think about him. But he made me laugh and he drove me home and he didn't ask about my seizure.

I drift off to sleep, the ghost of marshmallow and chocolate on my tongue.

CHAPTER
SEVEN

Sunlight streams through my bedroom windows when I wake to the smell of fresh coffee and pancakes. I text Mac before getting out of bed.

Tess: **You up?**

She responds with the green nausea emoji.

Mac: **I'm never drinking again.**
Tess: **Your mom called my mom. Are you grounded?**
Mac: **For the rest of my life.**
Tess: **That sucks.**
Mac: **I know. We should've just stayed at Seth's.**

Wait, what? Even if I'd told my parents I was sleeping at Mac's house, Mom's so anxious right now, she would have totally called the Bravermans to check on me. We'd be in the exact same situation we are now, only I'd be grounded, too. Before I can respond, Mac sends another text:

Mac: **Rachel and Simone did it. A whole bunch of people slept over. Seth's parents don't get home till tonight.**

Tess: You're not actually blaming me for this, are you?

Mac: **Well, it wasn't my idea to stroll through my living room while my mom was still awake.**

Tess: What was I supposed to do? Leave you passed out on the front porch?

Three dots waver, then disappear. Then waver again.

Mac: **Whatever. Let's just drop it. It is what it is.**

I toss my phone down without texting her back.

Dad's reading the paper at the kitchen table and Mom's flipping pancakes. "Morning," she says, as I fill a mug.

"Morning," I grunt, hunching over the steaming coffee. I can't believe Mac would actually blame me for what happened last night. She's the one who dragged me to that stupid party in the first place and then decided to get hammered, knowing full well she was our ride home. It sucks that she got grounded, but so many worse things could've happened last night. Mac and I used to make fun of classmates whose stories of hangovers and hookups cycled through Oakwood's rumor mill. But while I was judging, was Mac secretly wishing she was one of them?

Mom brings me two pancakes, whole wheat and hard as hockey pucks. "How's Mac this morning?" she asks, as though reading my mind.

"Beats me." Hard pass on having this conversation with my mom.

She pushes the syrup toward me. "You haven't had her over in a while. Everything okay with you two?"

"Mom. Everything's fine, okay? God."

Dad folds back the paper, shooting Mom a warning look. "Hon."

"What?" she snaps. "My kid gets busted for drinking and I'm not allowed to ask a few questions?"

"I told you I wasn't drinking!"

"She wasn't drinking," Dad says.

"Mac was, and that's not like her. I'm allowed to ask questions about our children's friends, Rob."

"Mooommm..." I groan.

A loud knock at the door interrupts us.

Dad puts down his paper.

"You expecting anyone?" Mom asks.

"Nope," he says. "Maybe the neighbors smelled your pancakes and came to check on us."

Mom swats him with a dish towel, the tense moment fizzling as he goes to answer the door.

A familiar voice trails in, and I freeze mid-chew. "Tess," Dad says, coming back into the kitchen. "It's for you. Says he knows you from the pool?"

"Have you even looked at me this morning?" I wave my arms frantically. "I'm not fit for human viewing! I'm not even wearing a bra!"

Dad blinks. "What do you want me to do? Send him away?"

"I don't know!"

"Is this the young man that drove you home last night?" Mom asks. "I'd like to talk to him."

"Mom, no!" I stand up so fast, my thighs slam against the table.

She puts down the spatula. Dad just stands there looking bewildered.

"It's just that you can be kind of...scary...sometimes."

"Me? I'm not scary!" She looks to Dad for affirmation. His right eye twitches—his most obvious tell.

59

"Look, whatever, okay? Just...stay here." On my way to the door, I grab a blanket off the couch, clutching the corners in front of my chest. My hair looks like I took a stroll through a wind tunnel, not to mention the raccoon circles under my eyes and my unbrushed teeth.

Charlie stands on my front porch. His hair's damp, and he smells cool and clean, like he just got out of the shower.

"Wow," he says, taking in my appearance.

I shut the door behind me. "What do you want?"

"Good morning to you, too."

I stare at him, and he clears his throat. "I was hoping we could try again."

"What are you talking about?"

"Breakfast," Charlie fumbles. "Pancakes? Or did I dream that for about half a second last night, you agreed to let me take you out?"

"I look like crap."

"Not possible."

Goosebumps prickle my skin, and I wrap the blanket tighter around my shoulders. "I was going to go for a run."

Charlie quirks his brow.

"Later I mean. My mom just made breakfast. Pancakes, actually."

"Coffee, then." The tips of Charlie's ears are shiny and pink. "I hope you don't have any more excuses because I barely have a shred of dignity left."

A smile blooms, unbeckoned. "Her pancakes are pretty bad. Whole wheat, even."

Charlie's face contorts in disgust. "Sacrilege."

"I could go for some real breakfast," I say.

"Good, because I actually don't even like coffee."

I laugh. "Give me five minutes."

When I poke my head into the kitchen, my parents grab their forks and pretend to eat. I roll my eyes. "I'm going to hang out with Charlie for a little while, okay?"

"Shouldn't he come in and meet us first?" Dad asks.

"You just met him a minute ago."

"You know what I mean."

"I haven't met him yet," says Mom.

"Look, could we please not make a big deal out of this? It's not like we're going on a date."

Mom pokes at a pancake. "Fine. But if he wants to take you out again, he's coming inside first."

Upstairs, I throw on cutoffs and a clean T-shirt and brush my hair into a ponytail.

Charlie's waiting outside in his Jeep, another classic rock tune blaring from his speakers, definitely not ironically.

"Could you at least turn it down?" I ask, climbing into the passenger seat. "I don't want my neighbors to think I'm getting kidnapped by a sixty-year-old."

Charlie laughs. "Just working on your musical literacy. Where's a good place to get breakfast around here? I'm starving."

"Let's try Billy's," I say, giving Charlie a few quick directions. "Best pancakes around."

"Now you're speaking my language." Charlie turns the music up as we pull away from my house.

———

The plate of pancakes in front of Charlie is bigger than his head. He also ordered eggs, sausage, and home fries, and has already plowed through most of it. "This place is amazing," he says, loading his fork again. A little bit of everything—the perfect bite.

"I eat like that, too," I tell him. "My sister teases me about it, because when I was little, the food on my plate couldn't touch, or I'd freak. I guess I was pretty uptight as a kid."

"You say that like you've changed," Charlie says.

I know he's teasing, but after the way Mac acted this morning, the comment stings, and I don't return his smile.

"Hey," he says, wiping his mouth. "I'm just messing around."

"Just because I'm not a party girl doesn't mean I don't know how to have fun."

"I know. I'm not really down for parties either—unless they involve cake and singing."

"Then why were you even there last night?"

"Hoping to meet people, I guess."

That makes my heart squeeze a little. Charlie always seems so comfortable. It's easy to forget he's the new guy in town.

"Look, I get that I don't know you that well," he says, mouth curling into a sheepish grin. "Clearly not well enough to tease you. But I know I'd like that to change."

I pluck invisible lint from my T-shirt, inching down my guard. "Why'd you guys move here anyway?"

"Apparently, sole custody of my little brother wasn't enough. Mom wasn't satisfied until we crossed state lines. Not that I blame her. We're staying with my aunt until we can find something permanent."

Lots of people I know have divorced parents, but most people see them both—even spend weekends and summer vacation swapping back and forth between houses. "It had to be hard leaving behind your friends and stuff."

"I mean, most people move away after senior year. But yeah. It hasn't exactly been the summer I was expecting."

"That I can relate to." I take a sip of coffee, swishing the bitter tang between my teeth. "My seizure cost me my job, my freedom, and a week of training. And the one person I thought I could count on for support is acting like a ... Rachel."

Charlie's thick brows knit together. "I don't follow."

I explain how Mac has seemed distant for weeks, but more so since my seizure, repeatedly blowing me off to spend time with Rachel, and how last night's performance was a side of her I've never seen. "She actually blames me for getting busted."

"I'm sure she's just pissed at herself," Charlie says. "It's easier to take it out on you."

I scowl. "That's so immature."

"People change sometimes, and not always for the better."

The bitterness in his voice takes me off guard, but before I can respond, a waitress pauses by our table, coffeepots in hand.

"Regular or decaf?" she asks.

"Decaf," I say.

"And another Coke for me, please," Charlie adds.

"Anything else?"

"Can I get a slice of apple pie?" Charlie asks. "You have pie, right?"

"You want dessert after everything you just ate?" I gape.

"I was hoping you'd share it with me." His wide hand dwarfs his cup, the fleeting darkness replaced by an earnest smile that softens my resolve.

"If it comes with vanilla ice cream and caramel syrup, I'm in."

"Can you make that happen?" Charlie asks the waitress.

She gives a curt nod before sauntering away.

"I wouldn't worry about Mac," Charlie says. "She's hungover and not thinking clearly. Tomorrow will be different, you'll see."

I muster a smile, thinking *different* is the problem and what I want is the same best friend, same job, same body as I had a few weeks ago, before my seizure, before this crap summer began.

The waitress returns with Charlie's refill and a wide slice of gooey apple pie, so warm the creamy scoop of ice cream covered in caramel syrup is already soft around the edges. "Lucky girl," she says. "This one's a catch."

"Oh, I'm not…We're not…" I fumble for the right words, but the waitress just winks at Charlie over her shoulder.

"I think she likes you," I tell him.

"Of course she does," Charlie teases. "I'm a catch."

His flashing dimple tugs a laugh from my chest. Until his eyes are too green and they're looking at me for too long.

I grab a spoon and plunge it into the pie, scooping up apples, ice cream, and just the right amount of caramel syrup.

Perfect.

———

Ali's on the couch with a blanket pulled up to her chin and a mug in her hands. "Where were you?" she asks, glancing up from the TV.

"I could ask you the same question," I snap.

"What?"

"I tried to call you like three times last night. You didn't answer any of my texts. I had to sneak Mac into her house, and we both got busted."

Ali palms her forehead. "I must've forgotten to charge my phone!"

"Seriously, Al? I thought you were here to help, not make everything worse."

"It was an accident, Tess, geez."

"How many times have I covered for you in the past?"

"You never—"

"That time you got locked out of your own window, so you climbed back in through mine." I count the memories on my fingers. "That time I had to keep Dad out of the living room so your loser boyfriend could leave. Oh, there was that other time—"

"Okay, okay!" Ali laughs. "You're right. I'm sorry. I should've been there for you and I wasn't. It will never, ever happen again. Happy?"

I huff.

"What did Mom and Dad say?"

"Oh, you know, just that I could have completely undermined my entire future. No biggie."

Ali snorts. "Leave it to Mom to make you feel like crap about your life choices." She tucks her legs to make room for me on the couch, and I sink down beside her.

"Where are they, by the way?" I ask.

"Errands. Mom asked if I wanted to come, but I needed a break. Caffeine before any more judgment."

"That bad, huh?"

"I've been here four days, and between the sideways barbs about living in the city and the casual mentions that 'it's never too late to go back to school,' I'm already beginning to question my sanity in coming back here."

I was in eighth grade when Ali announced over Dad's lasagna that community college wasn't for her. She was moving to New York to pursue an acting career. For the weeks that followed, until Dad rented a U-Haul so we could caravan into the city with Ali's bed and dresser in tow, my mom and sister were like angry bees, swarming around each other and stinging anyone that got in their way. Dad said they fought so hard because they love each other so much, but I wasn't sure—until Mom stepped foot into Ali's dusty one-bedroom efficiency and burst into tears.

"It's always been her way or the highway," Ali says, "but she's in rare form."

"Tell me about it. I mean, I get that swimming is more me and Dad's thing, but now, it's almost like she'd rather I just quit the team altogether."

"She's scared," says Ali. "It's stirring up all the crazy."

I laugh.

"I'm serious. At my age, Mom was clipping diaper coupons while Dad looked for a job. Her dreams weren't any bigger than a steady nine-to-five, food on the table, and a roof over their heads."

My eyes flick to the wedding picture hanging on the wall above the TV. Two-year-old Ali with her basket of flowers poses with my beaming, baby-faced parents, one year after a knee injury ended my dad's college football career and derailed his plan to go pro.

"She just doesn't get how that kind of safety doesn't necessarily equal happiness." Ali takes a sip of her coffee. "At least not for me."

"Or me," I say.

"Clearly," my sister teases. "Otherwise you wouldn't be sneaking around to ragers like some kind of rebel party animal."

"Shut up." I elbow her.

Ali laughs. "How was the party anyway? You know, before the getting busted part."

My mind drifts back to the warm glow of a firepit and the lingering taste of apple pie.

"Well...there's this guy."

Ali snuggles closer. "Tell me everything."

CHAPTER
EIGHT

When Mac picks me up for practice Monday morning, she wears an old baseball cap pulled low, and she's quiet when I get in the car.

"You okay?" I try.

"Depends on how you define *okay*," Mac says. "Other than practice and work, I'm basically on lockdown for the next two weeks."

"Could've been worse. Two weeks isn't terrible."

"Easy for you to say. You didn't get grounded."

"Yeah, because I wasn't drinking."

"Of course not," Mac grumbles. "I mean, you're in training, right? Can't let anything hold back mighty Tess Cooper." Her mocking tone has teeth; it nips at my patience.

"Look, I didn't do anything but make sure you got home safe, which I hope you would do for me. So what exactly is your problem?"

Mac's fingers flex around the steering wheel, knuckles white. "All I wanted was one fun night, but you couldn't even give me that."

"I went, didn't I? It's not my fault you got wasted."

"I know that, okay?" Mac squeezes the bridge of her nose. "It's just—do you even think about it?"

"What?"

"That night. At Rachel's."

"Not if I can help it."

"I can't stop." Mac's haunted eyes find mine. "You turned blue. Did you know that?"

"Mac," I warn. She's cracked a door I don't want to look through, not this morning, not on my way back to the water.

She presses on, the words untethered. "I held your head above water for as long as I could, but you started to turn blue, and I thought you were going to die right there, right in my arms."

"Stop," I plead.

Mac erases tears with a rough swipe of her palm. "When I saw you in the hospital, it was like I could breathe again. Like everything was going to be fine because you were alive. But all you care about is getting back in the water. Like it never happened." Her chin trembles. "Like it won't ever happen again."

"It won't," I say, the assurance in my voice pushing past my own creeping doubt. Today was supposed to be the first day of getting back to normal, but the glimpse backward has shaken me. I need Mac to convince me I won't have another seizure—not the other way around.

She sighs, emptied. "I just wanted to forget, you know? To have fun, for once in this fucked-up summer. To just be you and me without your seizure between us."

"Me too! But you went off with Rachel."

"For one game," Mac protests. "When I came back, you were gone."

"What did you expect me to do? Sorry for finding someone who actually wanted to spend time with me."

"I wanted to spend time with you! But you..." She shakes her head.

"What?" I demand. I wait for her to tell me I'm not fun enough; I don't want to play beer pong or sneak out at night, or do any of the things that suddenly seem so important to Mac.

"Never mind," she says. "Let's just drop it, okay?"

"Mac—" The word reaches out like grasping hands that come back empty.

"I said drop it." She turns up the music and we ride the rest of the way in silence.

———

At school, when we walk into the locker room, I feel like I'm in one of those "new kid" movies, where time slows down and everyone turns around to stare. Whispers scurry around the room like mice. My cheeks turn the same color as the hot-pink cap in my swim bag.

"Did you tell anyone what my doctor said?" I ask Mac as we change for practice.

"No, but they're going to find out anyway."

"I guess." It's not like my restrictions are a secret. But other than Coach and my family, Mac's the only person I've talked to about them. She did tell Rachel about my job at the Sugar Shack. How many other times has she talked about me behind my back?

Mac slides her goggles over her cap. "See you out there."

Davis greets me outside of the locker room. "Higgins wants you down here," he says, guiding me to the first lane, where a couple of freshmen usually swim. "Stick with freestyle and keep an aerobic pace," he instructs. "Take it easy, and let me know if it's too much."

This is what I promised, but the empty lane feels embarrassingly unnecessary. I belong in the center lane, next to Rachel and Mac, our speed propelling each other forward.

As my body moves through the motions of freestyle—reach,

pull, breathe, reach—the water washes away the events of last week. But 800 meters in, I start to get bored. While my teammates power through a pace workout that leaves them breathless and energized, I slog back and forth through the water for the entire two hours.

Normally by the end of practice, my breath is ragged, my heart slamming against my chest, and my brain floating on a cloud of endorphins. Today, my skin feels like a pair of polyester pajamas—itchy and ill-fitting.

"How'd that feel?" Coach asks as I hoist myself out of the pool.

I pull off my goggles. "Slow."

Around us, my teammates collect their gear and head back to the locker room where they'll change for lifting. "Hurry up," Davis calls, herding the freshmen stragglers. "Gym. Ten minutes!"

Coach taps her fingers against her clipboard. "I think dry land might be too much for you today."

"Coach," I protest. "I'm fine!" I'm more than fine—I'm barely winded, and the idea of box jumps and burpees feels like just what my body is craving.

"You won't be fine if you have another seizure." Coach's voice is a hard line. "You're back here tonight. Ease in. We can add lifting next week."

Words press hard against my lips, spilling out before I have time to consider the consequence. "When Mac had strep throat last winter, you didn't take it easy on her. And what about Simone? She swam through a foot fracture! It shouldn't be any different for me. My accommodations are for the water—not the gym."

"This isn't a debate, Tess," Coach says. "It's my way or nothing, got it?"

"Got it." I clamp my jaw as she taps her clipboard against the side of my arm.

"See you tonight."

Across the pool, Rachel whispers something in Mac's ear, then glances over her shoulder at me. Bitterness rises in my throat. Mac said she'd wanted one night to just be us—without the constant reminder of my seizure. But while she witnessed the worst thing that ever happened to me, I'm the one living its twisted aftermath. So how can she make this all about herself?

―

The pool hasn't opened yet when Ali drops me off for work. Charlie stands at the deep end, skimming a few fallen leaves. "Hey, Tess!" he calls.

I wave awkwardly, my phone in one hand and the iced coffee Ali bought me in the other.

Charlie puts down the skimmer and jogs over. Faint sleep lines cross his cheek, and his hair sticks up all over the place. "I didn't know you were working today. We could've ridden in together."

"Thanks, but my lazy sister needed to get up anyway."

"Better than the opposite. Max had the whole house awake by seven."

A sweet image rises: Charlie dozing on the couch while his little brother eats dry cereal and watches cartoons, like me and Ali used to do. "Seven a.m.," I say with a smirk. "That's brutal."

"What time does one of the best swimmers in the country wake up for practice?"

"Five."

Charlie whistles. "Now *that's* brutal."

I head for the Sugar Shack, and he jogs after me. "Seriously, though, we should ride in together when our schedules work. Doesn't make sense for two cars to drive the same route." He scratches the back of his neck. "You know, better for the environment and all that."

"Sure," I say, grinning at him. "Fewer emissions."

"It's the responsible thing to do."

A laugh bubbles out, and I look away, shaking my head. "I don't even have your number."

"That's definitely something we should change." Charlie reaches for my phone.

A warm, fluttery feeling spreads across my chest as I slide open the screen and hand it over.

"Better for the environment," he says, tapping in his number, "and cheaper than Uber."

Sara shouts at us from across the pool. "I'm not paying you two to stand around and flirt. We open in fifteen minutes."

I snatch back my phone and dart into the Sugar Shack before Charlie sees my cheeks suddenly match his red swim trunks.

CHAPTER
NINE

A few days pass before I take Charlie up on his offer. Ali's got an interview at a swanky new bakery this morning; Mac's off work, and things still feel too strained between us to ask for a favor. At work yesterday, with her in the guard stand and me in the Sugar Shack, it was easy to pretend we're fine. But other than a mumbled "thanks" when I'd offered gas money on the way home from practice, we barely spoke at all.

My stomach flip-flops around my avocado toast as I thumb a text to Charlie:

Tess: **Are you working today?**
Charlie: **Who wants to know?**

Here's what I want to type: *Wrong number. Never mind. You can go ahead and delete this text.* But I still need a ride to work, and so I take a deep breath and tell him it's me.

A laughing emoji pops onto my screen.

Charlie: **JK. Need a ride?**

I'm not sure if I'm relieved or want to throw my phone across the kitchen. I choose the former.

Tess: **If that's okay. I have to open.**
Charlie: **Mind leaving a little early? I have to make a stop on the way.**
Tess: **That's fine.**
Charlie: **See you in ten.**

Crap. I fly upstairs and into the bathroom, strip off my shirt, and splash water under my arms. I'm working the soap into a lather when Ali stumbles in, a sequined sleep mask pushed to her forehead. She blinks in the bathroom light. "What the—"

"I'm getting picked up in, like, two minutes. I don't have time for an actual shower."

She hikes up her T-shirt and drops onto the toilet. Her voice is thick with sleep. "Who's driving you?"

"Charlie."

Ali gives me a sleepy smile.

"He's just doing me a favor. It's not a big deal." I can tell by my sister's face she doesn't believe me, and neither do the neurotic butterflies swarming around in my gut.

"Char-lie and Te-ess, sitting in a..." Ali's pee is the tinkling background music of that stupid song.

"Shut up."

I've barely had time to change my shirt and grab a power bar when my phone chirps.

Charlie: **Here.**

Charlie waves at me when I step outside. There's a dark-haired guy in the passenger seat who waves, too. He has Down syndrome and looks roughly Charlie's age.

"Morning, sunshine!" Charlie croons. He's wearing dark sunglasses, but they can't hide the sleep lines that run down his cheek. His hair is crazy as usual, and an open can of Coke sits in his cupholder. "This is my cousin, Howie. Howie, meet Tess."

Howie sticks out his hand in greeting, and when I take it, he moves it to his lips and gives my knuckles a gentle peck. "Morning, sunshine," he says.

I laugh. "Nice to meet you, too."

"Howie works at the YMCA," Charlie says. "I told my aunt we'd drop him off on the way."

I buckle my seat belt and pull my hair into a ponytail at the base of my neck. "You just wake up?"

"I didn't sleep great last night," Charlie says. "So I slept in this morning." He gives me a sly smile through the rearview. "You know, that's something us mortal beings do when we're tired."

I punch his shoulder.

"I figured you could pick the music this morning." He unplugs the auxiliary cable from his phone and hands it to me. "Since classic rock clearly isn't your thing."

For some reason, sharing my playlist feels a little like letting Charlie take a peek in my underwear drawer. It's a glimpse at my inner workings, who I am when I'm excited, vulnerable, or sad. Music is what makes people tick—sharing it is like letting someone see the gears.

I choose a pretty benign tune, an acoustic indie, the kind I play in the background while I'm studying or doing homework.

Charlie listens intently, his fingers finding the song's undercurrent, tapping it out on the steering wheel. Howie's head bobs to the rhythm.

"Not bad," Charlie says when the song's over. "I totally had you pegged for, like, classical music, or I don't know, angry metal or something."

"Seriously?"

"You don't exactly scream top 100. And you clearly don't share my taste in music."

"Because the only people that do are fifty years old."

"Howie likes my music, don't you, Howie?"

Howie gives a half-hearted shrug. "Eh."

"You guys are the worst!" Charlie says, reaching for the cord. "Give me that back! You lost your turn."

At a red light, he shuffles through his phone, muttering to himself. "Here—everybody likes Steve Miller Band."

The opening chords of "The Joker" croon from the speakers, drawing the eyes of the driver next to us. Charlie belts out the lyrics like he's doing karaoke.

I don't sing. Not even in the shower. So when Charlie and Howie start swapping a pretend microphone at each chorus, sweat prickles the backs of my knees. Charlie hands me the "microphone," and I push his hand away. But he's persistent, until finally, I say, not sing, "Ooh wee, baby. I'll sure show you a good time."

Howie claps, and Charlie cheers, his dimple so deep, I want to press my finger into it.

By the time we arrive at the YMCA, I've almost forgotten we're headed to work. I'm just glad I got to spend time with Charlie.

"Thanks for the ride," Howie says, climbing out of the Jeep. "Three o'clock, right?"

"I'll be here," Charlie assures him.

"You're on pickup, too?" I ask.

"Nah. I'm teaching a swim class for kids with Down syndrome," Charlie says. "Howie roped me into it—he can be very convincing."

I laugh. "I bet."

"Hanging out with him is one of the best parts of living here." Charlie turns up the music, his singing lost in the wind as the Jeep picks up speed.

What would it be like to ditch work and drive all the way to the shore? For a second, I let myself imagine lying on the sand next to Charlie, soaking in the heat and not worrying about anything. But it's just a ride to work. And we're just friends. As Charlie belts out lyrics, his fingers drumming the beat, I can't help but wonder what it would be like if we were more.

—

I spend the morning doing inventory, counting chips and cookies while Taro, who's supposed to be helping, works on a new TikTok. I'm making a Costco list when Charlie takes his break. Standing in the guardhouse doorway, he stretches his long arms overhead, accentuating the sharp angles of his shoulders and biceps.

"I know, right?" says Taro.

My hand jerks so fast I smudge ink across the page.

Taro rests his chin dreamily on his fist. "I mean, he's totally a narp. But damn."

When Charlie starts in our direction, Taro and I turn away so fast, we almost bump into each other. And then I remember I'm supposed to be making a grocery list, so I do my best to focus on the word *pretzel* instead of Charlie's chiseled torso.

"Hey," he says.

Super casual, like I just noticed his presence: "Oh, hey."

From the back of the snack bar, where he's trying to hide behind the chips, Taro laughs.

"I was wondering if you wanted to go out again. For more pancakes?" Charlie's voice curves up around the word like he's not sure if he's saying it right. "Looks like we're both off tomorrow."

"You checked the schedule?"

Charlie's ears tinge pink. "I did—not like that's weird."

A smile teases up the corner of my mouth. I want to say yes, but my EEG is tomorrow, and I'm definitely not bringing that up in front of Taro. "I can't. I have a thing."

"Dinner, then?"

"I would, but I have practice."

Charlie looks appalled. "On Friday nights?"

"And Saturday mornings."

"That should be illegal."

"Preach," says Taro.

Charlie tugs on his earlobe. "Dinner Saturday? Final offer."

No matter how hard I try to convince myself Charlie and I are just friends, hanging out with him makes me feel like I just stepped off the Gravitron, that carnival ride that spins you around so fast, you're not sure which end is up.

Taro clears his throat dramatically.

"Okay, okay," I say. "It's a date."

"It's a date," Charlie echoes, flashing slightly crooked teeth.

I bite back a giddy smile as he walks away, and immediately grab my phone to text Mac.

Tess: **OMG. Charlie just asked me out!!!**

Mac's response is a string of fire emojis, and it's so Mac-like that relief rushes over me. Maybe we just need some time, just the two of us, when we're not rushing to practice or work, to talk this out. I offer a cautious olive branch: **Let's hang out this week?**

At first, Mac doesn't respond, and then:

Mac: **I'm grounded, remember?**

I shove my phone back in my pocket, trying to ignore the sag of disappointment. Later, then, once Mac's free. We'll get through this. We always do.

Charlie heads back to the guard stand, and Taro bumps me with his elbow. "Monday morning I'm going to need all the tea," he says.

I roll my eyes, but then Charlie turns around and waves, and it's the Gravitron all over again.

———

"So what kind of things do you like to do when you're not at school?" the EEG technician asks. It's another arbitrary question, designed to distract me from the scraping and gluing happening on my scalp. The electrodes she's attaching will track any electrical discharges in my brain over the next hour. I feel like a science experiment.

"I'm a swimmer," I tell her. "I'm headed to Northern Hills University next year."

"Well, isn't that nice," the tech says. Her neon-orange nails flutter above my head as she turns to the cabinet for more glue. "Both of my boys play baseball. Don't tell them I said this, but it's about as boring as watching paint dry."

Mom chuckles.

"Just a few more to go," the tech says. I turn my head sideways on the thin pillow so she can attach the final electrodes to the base of my skull. Then she explains how the test will work.

"I'm going to step outside, but you'll be able to hear my voice through an intercom. You'll need to follow my instructions exactly."

She tells me I'll need to breathe in and out through my mouth in short, quick huffs for four minutes. "Like this," she says, illustrating the sound, kind of like how women in the movies breathe during childbirth. "Then you'll see a series of flashing lights above you. After that, just close your eyes and do your best to relax."

"Do you want me to stay?" Mom asks.

"Yes, please." Maybe it's dumb, but I don't want to be alone.

The tech turns off the lights on her way out. The intercom clicks on, and her disembodied voice floats above me. "Remember, just try to relax."

Nothing about this is relaxing; my chest tightens as worries flood in. What if I have to keep taking these stupid safety precautions? I'll never make the A Finals at Nationals on a modified training schedule. Failing this test could even mean losing my scholarship. Mac will go away to college, and I'll be stuck here in Oakwood forever, dreaming about a professional swimming career I'm never going to have.

The click of the intercom interrupts my swirling thoughts. "We're going to start the breathing portion now. Remember, in and out through your mouth only." The tech huffs and puffs into the microphone. "I'll let you know how much time has passed. Go ahead and start."

Quick breaths—in and out. After a while, the back of my throat starts to itch. When is she going to tell me to stop?

"You're doing great, Tess. It's been one minute. Keep it up."

One freaking minute? What if breathing like this makes me have an actual seizure? Does the tech even know CPR?

I grip the sides of the bed, forcing myself to calm down. This is nothing but a breathing exercise. I'm under the tarp, and I'll be out soon. No big deal.

My body doesn't believe me.

"Two minutes. Great job."

Tingling panic rushes like water from the top of my head down to my toes.

"I can't," I gasp.

"It's okay," the tech says. "Just please try and stay calm."

Calm? My brain can't even register the word. I try to sit up, but the wires glued to my head yank me back down. "I can't do this, okay? I'm done."

Mom hurries over. "You're okay, honey. I'm right here."

My eyes burn, and I feel like an idiot. There's nothing to be afraid of. I've never failed a test in my life. Mom wipes a rogue tear from my cheek, and I concentrate on the steady rise and fall of my belly button, the rush of air in and out of my lungs.

The tech checks to make sure all the electrodes are still attached. Mom pulls her chair across the room so she's sitting right beside me.

"Everything's going to be fine," she whispers, for once sounding more like Dad than herself. That's how I know she's lying.

CHAPTER
TEN

I'm standing in front of my open dresser drawer, wearing only my bra and underwear, and trying to decide what to wear to dinner with Charlie tonight. The last time we went out, I was barely decent—still stinking of the party the night before. This is a real date with potential for date-like things, like end-of-the-night kisses and worrying if he'll call.

Ali sticks her head in my room without knocking. "I convinced Dad to order in. What sounds good, Chinese or pizza?"

"I'm going out," I tell her, yanking on a striped T-shirt and a pair of jeans.

"With Mac?"

"With Charlie."

My sister makes a noise like helium escaping the mouth of a balloon. "You have a date? Please tell me that's not what you're wearing."

"What's wrong with this?"

"Nothing if you're playing mini golf." Ali spits out the words like they taste bad. She heads to my closet, rifling through my sweaters and the few dresses I own, emerging with a fluttery romper. "Sexy with a pair of wedges, right?"

"What's the verdict?" Dad calls from the bottom of the stairs.

"Tess has a date!" Ali yells back.

I gape at her, and she smirks.

"A date?" Dad echoes.

I head to the top of the stairs, shoving my sister out of the way. Dad's barefoot in his uniform, his forehead pink from a day delivering mail in the sun.

"It's just dinner."

Mom joins Dad at the bottom of the stairs. "Dinner with who?"

"Charlie." Ali jiggles the hanger. "Don't you think she should wear this?"

"Would you shut up?" I hiss.

"Isn't that the boy that drove you home from the party the other night?" Mom asks.

"Yes, but—"

"I hope he's planning on coming inside this time," Dad says.

Ali has single-handedly eviscerated any hope I'd had of downplaying my plans, hopefully sparing Charlie the what-are-your-intentions-with-my-daughter talk. I jerk the romper out of her hand and stalk into my bedroom.

"Can I at least curl your hair?" Ali begs. "It looks so pretty in curls."

I shut the door in her face. My hands tremble a little as I twist open a tube of mascara. "Get it together," I tell my reflection. "It's just Charlie."

That works for about two seconds, right up until the doorbell rings.

I dart down the steps, nearly steamrolling my sister, who's already reaching for the doorknob. "Can everybody just be normal please?"

Dad gives an apprehensive nod, like normal is a state of being he's not usually in, but he'll give it a shot.

"If normal is introducing yourself to the young man taking your daughter out," Mom says.

"Nope," says Ali.

I open the door.

Charlie's on the front stoop, and with one look at him, I'm wishing I'd worn that stupid romper. He's wearing jeans, sneakers, and a button-down, which I'm kind of surprised he even owns. His hair's been styled with some kind of product that makes it look even more...messy.

"Hey."

"Hey," he says. "Ready?"

"My parents actually want to meet you." I open the door wider so he can see my family lined up in order of height. Ali gives a little wave. "Sorry."

Charlie grins, extending his hand first to my dad. "Nice to meet you, Mr. Cooper."

The meet and greet is relatively painless, except for when Mom quizzes Charlie on the statistics of teen death by drunk driving, and the few awkward minutes when Dad asks Charlie what he thinks about the Eagles' picks, and Charlie (clearly not a football fan) fumbles through a half-baked answer.

When we escape down the sidewalk, Ali leans out the door and calls after us, "You two crazy kids have fun now! Don't do anything I wouldn't do!"

"Nice family," says Charlie as we climb into the Jeep.

"You clearly haven't spent enough time with them."

———

The spicy sweet smells of teriyaki and wasabi greet us as we step inside Kyoto, an upscale sushi restaurant. Shiny green plants almost touch the ceiling in the corners of the room, heavy leaves tugging on narrow trunks. The hostess is dressed in sleek black pants and a silky blouse. My toes dig into my plain leather sandals, and I wish I'd at least painted my toenails.

The "Happy Birthday" song draws my attention to the back of the restaurant, where three servers serenade a table of teenage girls: Rachel, Lily, Simone, and Mac, who apparently isn't that grounded after all. A sparkler-lit dessert lights up Rachel's face. She struggles to blow it out while the other girls laugh and cheer.

I want to sink into the floor and disappear.

"Can we go somewhere else?" I whisper to Charlie.

"Sure, I guess," he says, "but why?"

I fumble for an answer, blurting out the first mostly true thing I come up with: "I'm not a huge fan of fish."

Charlie's ears ignite. "Oh! I should've asked—"

"I should've said something," I tell him, wishing I'd come up with a better reason to leave. "Let's go before they seat us."

"Well, now I feel bad," Charlie says in the parking lot, where the air smells like hot cement and hibachi smoke.

"Look at it this way: we just gave them an empty table for somebody who doesn't have a reservation."

Charlie looks doubtful. "I guess."

As we climb into the Jeep, I start to thumb a quick text to Mac.

Tess: **WTF. Grounded?**

"Everything okay?" Charlie asks.

I open my mouth to tell him Mac lied to me—just when it seemed we could mend. Then I realize she's having a fun night, and I'm not about to let her ruin mine. "Everything's fine," I tell him, offering a reassuring smile.

"Good," he says. "Any idea where we should go now?"

"Tacos. And I know the perfect place."

"This was a good call." Charlie licks sour cream from the corner of his mouth before taking another bite of his overstuffed taco.

We're the only people sitting in the metal chairs outside Paprika. The chili pepper lights overhead flicker red and green. A few cars drive by, but the quiet out here is a welcome relief from the noise in Kyoto. Best of all, it's Mac-and-Rachel-free.

"This place is my favorite," I say.

"I can see why." Charlie reaches for the basket of chips. "You know all the best places to eat around here. Screw Yelp—I should've just asked you."

"Yelp?"

"Kyoto had five stars," Charlie explains. "I wanted to take you someplace nice."

I bite into my taco, hoping he doesn't notice the pink flush creeping into my cheeks. "I am known for my fine taste in cuisine." A piece of lettuce escapes, and my hand flies to my mouth. Charlie cracks up.

"This place probably isn't even on Yelp," I say. "But it's definitely the best."

"Oakwood's best kept secret." His eyes hold mine, and for just a moment, I forget how to breathe.

After dinner, we stop for dessert at Sprinkles, a self-serve Froyo spot near our neighborhood. We load our cups with frozen yogurt, and when we move on to toppings, Charlie acts like a little kid in a candy store.

"Your chance of developing diabetes by the end of the night gets higher with every spoonful," I tell him as he adds M&Ms to the tiny mountain steadily growing higher in his cup.

Charlie drizzles chocolate syrup over his concoction and tops it off with a spiral of whipped cream. "Worth it."

We take our dessert to a small park across the street and settle into the swings.

"Want to trade bites?" Charlie holds out a spoonful dripping with chocolate sauce.

"Too sweet for you, huh?"

"No way—just thought you might want in on this."

My taste buds flinch at the sugar explosion. "Why didn't you just get all toppings?" I ask, thumbing chocolate from the corner of my mouth.

"I figured that was probably frowned upon in a frozen yogurt store."

"Want a bite of mine?" I let him dig his spoon into my cup. He makes sure to get a little bit of both flavors and some crushed Heath bar. The perfect combination.

"Mmm," he says, closing his eyes. "It tastes like a caramel Frap."

"Exactly." He moves in for seconds, and I bat his hand away. "Those suckers are my secret weakness."

"I didn't realize one of the best swimmers in the country had a weakness."

I let my swing fall away from Charlie's. "Turns out I do."

The narrow strip of space between us suddenly throbs with palpable energy. Charlie interrupts the silence. "Hey, speaking of, when do I get to see you swim?"

A meet might bore Charlie out of his mind. On the other hand, it would be a chance for him to see a little bit of my world. "There's a meet next weekend. You could come, if you want."

"Could I make a poster with your name on it?"

"Nope."

"Could I bring a bullhorn to cheer for you?"

"Absolutely not."

"Fine. I'll cheer quietly. To myself. But no promises on the poster."

"Does that mean you're coming?" I lick the back of my spoon, weirdly nervous about his answer, like I just asked him out on a date. Come to think of it, maybe I did.

"I wouldn't miss it."

Charlie bends over and puts his cup in the grass. Butterflies slam against my rib cage. Is he going to kiss me? How would you even kiss on a swing? Not that I don't want him to kiss me. I do, but it's been so long since I've been kissed, what if I do it wrong? What if he does it wrong? I need to do something, to move, to escape. So I ditch my ice cream and start swinging.

"Seriously?" Charlie asks. "This is what we're doing right now?"

"Yep." My legs pump faster, propelling me higher into the air. My hair whips against my cheeks. "Want to see who can get higher?"

"No thanks. Barfing on dates makes me uncomfortable."

"You say that like you've done it before."

Charlie sways forward and back. "Over three years of dating, I've accumulated quite the list of dos and don'ts."

"Speaking of which," I tease, "what *is* that stuff in your hair?"

His hand flies to his hair, patting it down. "You don't like my hair? My mom said I should"—he puts air quotes around the words—"'do something with it for once.'"

I skid to a stop, slightly nauseous. "I like your hair the way it usually is."

"Aw. You said you like me."

"I said I like your hair."

"Same thing."

"It is not…"

Charlie grabs my swing and pulls me around to face him. Smile lines crinkle the corners of his eyes. "I like you too, Tess."

Blood pulses in my fingers and toes. "Too bad I don't kiss on the first date."

"Who said I was going to kiss you?"

"Well, you were, weren't you?"

"I was thinking about it." Charlie lets go of my swing, and I fall backward, relief and disappointment prickling my skin. "But I don't kiss on the first date either."

For a minute, the only sound is our breathing and the rustling leaves of the trees overhead.

"I mean, it's technically not our first date." Embarrassment floods every nerve in my body, but my mouth won't stop moving. "We did go out to breakfast."

"And tonight was almost like two dates," Charlie muses. "So technically, we're on our third date. It's probably fine to kiss on the third date, right? If we wanted to, I mean."

"Yeah. If we wanted to."

Charlie reaches for my swing again. He twists me around to face him, his toes hooking behind my heels. "Do you want to?"

My breath hitches in my chest, and I nod.

"Good," he says, leaning forward. "So do I."

I close my eyes.

"Hang on a second."

My eyes fly open.

"This is kind of a high-pressure situation, being our first kiss and all."

Anticipation is an actual flavor in my mouth, caramel and chocolate and cookie crumbs. I know what I want now. My whole body surges toward it.

"I mean, it should be perfect," Charlie says. "What if I mess up?"

I can't wait any longer. I lean forward and press my mouth to

Charlie's. His body stiffens in surprise, and then I feel his smile against my lips.

It is perfect and imperfect. Soft lips and gentle tongues and teeth that touch a little. The moment washes over me like clear, clean water.

CHAPTER
ELEVEN

"That's her," I tell Ali when she drops me off for practice Monday morning. Rachel saunters across the parking lot sipping a Venti iced coffee; her orange convertible chirps as she locks it over her shoulder.

I'd told Ali what happened at Kyoto, and the text I'd sent Mac yesterday about seeing her while out with Charlie. Apparently, Mac's mom had granted her a one-night parole to celebrate Rachel's birthday. Still, the old Mac would've woken me up with a barrage of texts, begging for details about my date. This Mac never even asked.

"Want me to run her over?" Ali asks.

I smirk. "Rain check?"

Rachel greets me in the locker room. "We need details about the narp," she says, making it clear I've walked into the middle of a conversation—about me.

"He's so hot," Simone gushes.

"And I hear he likes sushi." Rachel's tongue peeks out from between perfect teeth.

Mac blanches.

I clutch my swim bag like a weapon and hurry to my locker.

"Relax." Rachel laughs. "We're just messing around."

"What the hell?" I hiss at Mac.

"I may have mentioned—" she tries, but Rachel interrupts her.

"If he took you to Kyoto, he's got good taste. Plus, if you tell them it's your birthday, you get free cake."

This is apparently hilarious, because Lily and Simone crack up on their way out to the pool. Rachel follows. "And a get-out-of-jail-free card." She winks at Mac as the door swings shut.

Mac is suddenly very interested in something deep inside her locker, but the flush creeping up her neck tells me all I need to know. "So it wasn't really her birthday?"

She shakes her head.

"Why would you lie to me?"

"It wasn't a lie," she protests. "More of an omission. I really did tell my mom that so she'd let me go out. I'm wasting my summer in Braverman jail, Tess. I was desperate."

"Just not desperate enough to hang out with me." My words have serrated edges; they cut the corners of my mouth.

"I'm sorry," Mac says. "I didn't think—"

I cut her off with a harsh laugh. "Pretty sure Rachel does the thinking for both you of these days."

Mac reels back. My anger and hurt are circling sharks: they move in for the kill. "You used to make fun of girls like that. Turns out you're just like them."

I slam my locker and storm out to the pool. Fury fuels my workout, but my mind remains unfocused, my body so heavy, it feels like I'm swimming through sand.

———

It's two a.m., and I can't sleep. Mac and I have barely spoken for two days. And in exactly seven hours, I'll find out the results of my EEG. It's open season for my brain, and worries whiz by like bullets. I text Ali.

Tess: **You up?**

Ten TikToks later, I figure the answer is no. My sister sleeps like a hibernating bear and is just as grumpy if you wake her up.

So I try Charlie.

Tess: **You awake?**
Charlie: **I thought I was the only one in the neighborhood up. Don't you have practice in an hour?**

An owl emoji pops onto the screen.

Tess: **Practice is in four hours. And yeah. It's gonna suck.**
Charlie: **Been up all night. Can I call you?**

Talking over the phone in the middle of the night seems like new territory for us. Especially when I'm lying in my bed, wearing a T-shirt and underwear. Oh my God, I'm not wearing pants.

My phone buzzes, and I panic, like Charlie can somehow see me. He's probably in bed, too. And then I wonder whether he's wearing pants and what his pillows smell like. I'm literally a walking hormone.

"Hey," he says, his voice distant and sort of muffled.

"Where are you?" I ask.

"I'm jogging."

"At two in the morning?"

"Yeah. I go jogging when I can't sleep. Do you want to come with me? You know, since you can't sleep either."

I have practice in the morning, and a night of no sleep could land me smack on Coach's shit list. But whether I go with Charlie or not, I still have to get up in a few hours. The exercise might clear my head and help me catch a little sleep before practice. "I'll meet you outside in five minutes."

It's weirdly bright out when I join Charlie in the yard, the moon a full white orb. Huck whimpers after me, so I grab his leash. He bounds over to Charlie and promptly flops onto his back for a belly rub, which Charlie generously supplies.

We start at an easy pace. My legs feel heavy with lack of sleep, but soon the movement stretches them awake. Our feet settle into a rhythm, pounding the pavement in perfect sync. Huck is still running point, not yet tired enough to drag behind me.

"How far do you usually run?" I ask.

"Until I get tired."

Charlie always looks so sleepy, always guzzling Coke. Maybe I'm not the only one running away from something.

"I think we should turn around up here," I say, pointing to the trail entrance ahead.

Charlie glances sideways. "You don't want to run the trail?"

"It's the middle of the night. Don't you think that sounds a little...unsafe?"

"You worried about bears?"

"More like axe murderers."

"I run this trail at night all the time, and I haven't seen one axe murderer. Plus, we've got Huck to protect us."

I snort, knowing full well that if we run into an axe murderer, I'll have to save all three of us.

At the trail entrance, the sidewalk gives way to gravel, and trees fill in around us. The air smells wet, like damp mulch. The silver moon shines through the canopy of leaves, casting soft gray light on the trail and shimmering on the surface of the wide creek alongside it.

Something scampers through the brush and scurries up a tree. Huck whines and strains against the leash, so I grip it tighter. The last thing I need is to lose him in the woods at night.

Charlie's pace is steady, but I keep up, even as sweat beads on my upper lip and my shirt starts to stick to my back. The exercise relaxes me—my worries disappear like ghosts through the trees. We swap lifeguarding horror stories, including the tale of "Shit Summer," which was even worse than its name.

"So if you've been lifeguarding all these years," I say, "how come you've never joined a swim team?"

"I did for a while when I was younger. But the meets were too long." Charlie gives me a sheepish grin. "I got bored."

"I'll try not to take that personally."

"I'm really looking forward to your meet, though. What do you swim?"

"A little of everything, but mostly freestyle. My best event is the 200-meter."

"End of the pool and back twice?"

I nod. "It's the perfect event. You have to pace yourself, but barely. The last lap is an all-out battle to the finish. It's where you figure out what you're made of."

"And how long does it take?"

"My best time was a little under one fifty-eight."

"One minute and fifty-eight seconds? That's pretty fast!"

"You're pretty fast, too," I say, picking up my speed. "Did you ever run track?"

Charlie shrugs off the thought. "I gave it a shot once, but everyone was so focused on impressing college recruiters—not for me."

"Don't you think about college?" Every senior at Oakwood

knows exactly where they're headed after high school. We've all been planning our futures since freshman year.

"I'm not against college," Charlie says. "But I figure I'll hang out here for a while, until my mom and Max get situated, and then see what's next."

"Doesn't not knowing stress you out?"

Charlie gives me a sideways grin. "Sounds like it stresses you out."

"I mean, a little." I think about the stack of books beside my bed, the SAT prep course I took not once, but three times, and the Northern Hills T-shirt I ironed before hanging in my closet. "Okay, a lot."

Charlie laughs, a low chuckle from deep in his chest.

"What's wrong with having a plan? If you don't know where you're going, how are you supposed to get there?"

"Maybe," Charlie muses, "but I like to keep my options open."

Huck drags behind me, and we still have a three-mile run home. "We have to turn around," I tell Charlie. "This guy's not going to make it much farther."

"Should we let him get a drink?"

"Good idea."

We pick our way through the brambles until our feet start to sink into the damp earth along the creek bed. Huck strains toward the water, and I loosen my grip on the leash. He lunges in, lapping with desperate thirst.

"How often do you jog at night?" I ask.

Charlie stretches his ankles against a nearby stone. "A few times a week. Whenever I can't sleep."

"Why can't you sleep?"

"Different reasons, I guess." Something hops into the water, making a small splash. Huck's ears perk up. "My dad called tonight."

"Is that…unusual?"

Charlie shrugs. "He actually calls a lot. I usually don't answer."

"Don't you miss him?"

Before Charlie can respond, Huck lunges. The leash jerks out of my hand, and my dog goes bounding into the creek, sending a spray of muddy water all over me and Charlie.

"Huck! Get back here!"

My crazy dog is joyfully frolicking in hip-deep water, nipping at invisible fish and frogs. Charlie thinks it's hilarious. "I'm going to have to go in after him," I say, slipping out of my shoes and tucking my phone safely inside.

"I'll help."

Even at this time of year, the water is freezing, and I suck in air through my teeth as the creek rises from my ankles to my knees, soaking the bottom of my shorts. We step gingerly across pebbles and stones until they give way to a soft bottom.

Huck barks happily and splashes over. By the time I finally get my hand under his collar and drag him out of the creek, Charlie and I are both soaked.

"Sorry about that." I wipe my eyes on the only dry spot left on my shirt. The smell of stale fish makes my lips curl. "So much for sneaking back into the house unnoticed."

"We could clean him up at my place," Charlie offers, ringing out his shorts.

"What about your mom?"

"My family's gotten pretty used to me jogging at night. As long as we're quiet, they won't think anything of it. We can hose him off and at least towel him dry before you take him home."

I check my phone—plenty of time to rinse Huck at Charlie's, get home, and maybe even snatch an hour of sleep before I have to get up for practice. My battery's low, and I make a mental note to charge it when I get home. "That sounds like our best option."

Huck, on the other hand, is ready for bed after a jog and a swim. No matter how hard I pull on the leash or how sweetly I cajole him, he refuses to run, and what should be a twenty-minute jog home turns into a cold, wet walk.

"My dad wants to see me," Charlie eventually tells me. "But I don't want to see him. That makes me feel like a jerk, you know? What kind of guy doesn't want to see his own dad?"

I slide my hand into Charlie's and squeeze. "I'm guessing you have a reason."

"Yeah." He interlaces his fingers with mine. "I don't like talking about my dad. But I do like talking to you."

"I like talking to you, too."

When we reach Charlie's house, we head straight to the back-yard to hose off Huck. Charlie dips inside for towels, then helps me dry him off.

"Do you want to come inside for a little while?" Charlie asks when we've finished. "We could watch a movie or something while he dries."

I don't bother checking the time. At this point, I'm better off staying awake and napping after practice. But I do have to get home before the coffee turns on—if my parents wake up and discover I snuck out in the middle of the night to see a boy, I'm dead. "I guess for a little while," I say.

Charlie's kitchen smells like something spicy—curry, maybe—and a child's drawings cover almost every inch of the fridge. He spreads out a towel for Huck, who immediately flops down, exhausted. "Hungry?" Charlie asks, opening the pantry.

We make a snack of apples and peanut butter and carry it to the living room. A string of twinkling white lights lines the larg-est window. Colorful woven blankets are slung across the worn brown couch, welcoming afternoon naps and movie dates, but my clothes are still soaked in creek water. Charlie glances down at his own wet clothes. "Want to borrow something dry?"

It does not escape me that this situation is straight out of a rom-com. If movie-me follows Charlie to his room, he'll offer me a clean T-shirt. I'll awkwardly tell him to turn around while I change, but the situation is so loaded with sexual tension we'll definitely end up making out in his bed. If Mac was here, she'd practically push me upstairs, but I'm not ready to be shirtless in Charlie's room. "I'll wait here."

"Good idea," he says. "Wouldn't want to wake up Howie and Pickles."

Heat floods my cheeks. "Oh."

Charlie jogs upstairs. The twinkle lights bathe the cozy room in soft light, and Huck's snores whistle from the kitchen. Exhaustion plows into me like a tsunami. I sink down onto the carpet and prop my head against a soft couch cushion. How long does it take to change clothes, anyway? Charlie should be downstairs any minute.

CHAPTER
TWELVE

A dog's bark nudges me into consciousness. A soft, faded quilt covers my body. Sun streams through the windows. It is well past five.

"Shit!" I sit straight up, pushing off the quilt and scrambling for my phone. The screen is blank, the battery dead. Charlie's asleep on the couch, his hair wet from the shower he must've taken while I slept on the floor. "Shit, shit, shit!"

Howie's standing in the kitchen in boxer shorts and a T-shirt, holding Pickles under one arm. The squirmy little rat snarls and scratches the air as Huck cowers behind the narrow kitchen table. "I didn't mean to wake you up," says Howie. "Pickles had to pee."

"It's okay." Bleary-eyed, I scan the cluttered kitchen for Huck's leash. "I shouldn't be here, anyway."

Howie's forehead creases. "Should your dog?"

"Definitely not." The clock says 7:15. Practice is half over, and my parents are probably freaking out by now. I'll be lucky if they haven't called the cops. I shove my feet into my shoes. "Let's keep this between us, okay, Howie?"

"My lips are locked."

"What time is it?" Charlie groans from the couch.

"Seven-fifteen. I totally slept through practice, and my parents have no idea where I am. I'm dead."

He sits up, rubbing a hand through his hair. "I'll drive you."

"I'll get there faster on foot." I push through the door, Huck on my heels. We're running before we even make it to the sidewalk.

My parents are pacing the living room when I burst through the door. Dad's wearing his work uniform, but Mom's still in her bathrobe. Relief floods her face, followed almost immediately by fury. "Where the hell have you been?"

I fumble for an excuse that doesn't involve falling asleep in a boy's living room, but Mom's not actually interested in what I have to say.

"I tried your phone; I tried Mackenzie's phone." Her eyes widen as she takes in my appearance, my disheveled ponytail and my mud-splattered clothes. "What in God's name..."

"I just went for a run," I say as Huck hurriedly escapes to the kitchen. "We took the trail by the creek, and he went after something in the water. It took me forever to get him. I would've called but my battery died."

"A run?" Mom exclaims. "And you went in the creek?" She taps her temples, like her brain is about to explode. "Do you even understand how dangerous that is? How careless? What if you'd had a seizure out there? You could have died, Tess. Do you realize that?"

There's movement on the staircase. Ali sits in her pajamas at the top, listening. Five years ago, it would've been me on the stairs and Ali in the living room, facing my parents' wrath after missing curfew or getting caught drinking. They'd take away her car keys, but the next morning everything would go back to normal—at least until she screwed up again. But my parents aren't going to get over my seizure.

Dad's face is etched with deep lines of worry. Normally, he does his best to buffer Mom's temper, but this morning, he's quiet, and the look on his face is worse than anger: he's disappointed. "This isn't like you, Tess."

"I'm really sorry, and I'll try to be more careful." I rush through the words I know they need to hear. Coach is probably fuming by now; a missed practice is the last thing I need. "Can I go change? If we hurry, I can still catch the last half of practice."

"Absolutely not," Mom huffs. "Dad was supposed to be at work thirty minutes ago, and your appointment's in a few hours. You have to learn how your actions affect other people, Tess. You're skipping the rest of practice."

"Wait, what?" I exclaim. "Dad?"

"Your mom's right," he says. "We were really worried about you. There has to be some kind of consequence. If my quarterback missed practice, he'd be on the bench, too."

"It was an accident! I would've called if I could. I'm right here, aren't I? I'm fine!"

"And thank God for that." When Mom's like this, there's no getting through to her. I push up the stairs past my sister and slam my bedroom door. This was a stupid, completely avoidable mistake. Dad's right; it's not like me at all.

———

Even guzzling coffee doesn't touch the cloud of exhaustion that hovers over me as I wait in Dr. Cappalano's office, scrolling through my phone just to stay awake.

Charlie: **Can we talk later?**
Tess: **Do we have to?** *Delete.*
Tess: **There's nothing to talk about.** *Delete, delete.*
Tess: **Only if there's kissing involved.** *Delete, delete, delete.*

It's not Charlie's fault that I missed practice this morning. Still, if I can't spend time with him and stay focused on swimming, I don't know how much further I want this to go.

"Tess Cooper?" A nurse stands in the waiting room doorway.

"That's us," Mom says, closing her magazine. Nerves prickle my skin like static, but I cling to a desperate thread of hope that only frays slightly when Dr. Cappalano walks into the exam room.

"It seems we have both good and bad news for you today," she says.

My fists clench and unclench against my thighs.

"Unfortunately, your EEG did show some spikes and sharp waves, particularly during the hyperventilation portion of the test. As I said before, EEGs are not fail-proof; however, these discharges are consistent with what we see in generalized epilepsy…"

The doctor continues speaking, her pink-ringed mouth still moving, her hands annunciating her sentences with random gesticulations. But my brain has stopped listening.

Epilepsy.

The word sucks my breath away, and suddenly, I'm underwater, but I can't swim and I can't find the surface and I can't breathe I can't breathe I can't breathe…

"Tess!" Mom grips my arms with icy hands. "Are you okay?"

"I have to get out of here," I wheeze.

Mom pushes back my hair, brushes her thumb across my cheekbone. "It's going to be okay, honey."

The flimsy paper on the exam table rips off in my hands.

"You said there was good news?" Mom asks the doctor.

"A person isn't diagnosed with epilepsy until they've had at least two seizures unprovoked by some other reversible medical condition," Dr. Cappalano says. "At this point, you've only experienced one. If or when you have another, this type of epilepsy usually responds well to medication, and there are several different options we could try."

"*That's* the good news?" I croak. "That I haven't had another seizure *yet?*"

"Unfortunately, that's the nature of this condition. We just don't know if you'll have another seizure until you do."

"What about swimming?"

Dr. Cappalano folds her hands in her lap. "People with epilepsy can live very normal lives as long as their seizures are controlled. If you're swimming now, I don't see why you can't continue with the modifications we discussed, as you long as you don't overdo it."

I don't want to live a normal life. Normal teenagers don't win national championships.

Mom tries to hug me, but I jerk away.

"Keep in mind that if you go a full six months without another seizure, you're less likely to have another," says Dr. Cappalano. "At that point, we can make a more informed decision about what's safe and what isn't. Let's just hope you never have another seizure again."

A lump rises in my throat and tears sting the corners of my eyes.

Hope is a dangerous thing.

———

Dad made lasagna. This, along with the fact that Mom let him, tells me all I need to know about my parents' reactions to my EEG results. I'm bracing myself for a family talk as I head downstairs for dinner.

There's a knock on the door. "I'll get it," I yell. Charlie's standing on the front stoop.

"I texted," he says, with a sheepish glance at my tank top and pajama shorts.

"Sorry," I say. "It's been a pretty shitty day."

"No, I'm sorry. I should've woken you up last night, but I just didn't think." His ears, shining red beacons, announce his rattled nerves, and my fingers twitch to tug his earlobe, to brush the sprinkling of stubble on his cheek. "Your parents probably hate me," he says, glancing past me into the house.

"They don't know I was with you," I whisper. "So don't go mentioning it to them."

"Noted." Charlie runs his foot across the dusty doormat. "So are we okay?"

I know what I should say—that I don't have time for a relationship, that I need to stay focused on my goals. Especially now.

But I can't. I look at Charlie's crazy hair, his soft green eyes, and his massive hands that touched my face so gently the night we kissed, and my heart swells with wanting. "Yeah. We're okay."

"Cool." Charlie scratches the back of his neck. "I'm free now if..."

"I'm in my pajamas!" I give him a playful shove.

He catches my hand and tugs me toward him, wrapping his arms around my lower back.

"Who is it?" Ali asks, and I slip out of Charlie's arms. "Oh, hey, Charlie. Are you staying for dinner?"

If my parents are gearing up for a talk about the future of my swimming career, I'd rather spare Charlie. "No, he was just—"

"Sure!" Charlie says. "I mean, if you want me to."

I offer a weak smile. "Sure. Come on in."

My parents are already seated. Huck bounds over to sniff Charlie's ankles, but my parents greet us with question marks on their faces.

"We need an extra plate," Ali announces.

"Hi, Charlie." Mom's voice is laced with hesitance. "I didn't realize you were coming for dinner."

"Neither did I," Charlie says. "I hope that's okay?"

My parents exchange a loaded look. They were definitely planning a family discussion, and I can only hope Charlie's presence has thrown a wrench in that plan. "Sure," Mom says. "We're glad to have you."

"I hope you like cheese," Dad says.

"Yes, sir." Charlie eyes the bubbling lasagna in the center of the table. "Big fan."

Dad grins. "I'll get another chair."

"How do you like the neighborhood so far?" Mom asks, passing Charlie the salad bowl.

"We really like it." He smiles at me. "Nice neighbors."

Ali smirks, and I kick her under the table.

"I met your mother the other day," Mom continues. "She had your brother out on his bike. Cute little boy."

Charlie grins over a forkful of lasagna. "Most of the time."

"It must be hard raising the two of you all by herself."

"Mom!" I exclaim.

"What?" Mom gives me a wide-eyed, innocent look. "I'm just making an observation—you two girls have been hard enough, and I had help."

"Thanks, hon," Dad says sarcastically.

"Oh, you know what I mean."

"I'm sure Charlie didn't come here to play twenty questions," Ali says. "Maybe you could lay off a little?"

"It's okay." Charlie wipes his mouth. "We do all right, Mrs. Cooper. I help out my mom a lot."

"See?" Mom says. "We're just having a conversation."

"Delicious lasagna, by the way," Charlie adds.

"Thank you." Mom points her fork at Dad. "But I can't take the credit."

"I'm the meat and cheese connoisseur," Dad says. "And I only get to cook a couple times a week."

"Which means we only eat a couple times a week," Ali chimes in.

"Hey!" Mom exclaims.

I let out a small exhale. So far, my family's actually acting pretty normal, and Charlie's inhaled his lasagna in under four bites. We might just get through this dinner before the conversation turns to me at all.

"So, Charlie," Dad says, "are you going to Central?"

Charlie's mouth is full, so I answer for him. "He graduated last May."

"Congratulations," Mom says. "What are your plans for the fall?"

Given my parents' feelings about college, this conversation is moving into dangerous territory.

Charlie swallows. "I'm actually still figuring that out."

"You don't have plans for college?" Mom's knife clicks against her plate.

"Not everybody has to go to college, Mom," Ali pipes up. "A lot of people do just fine without a degree."

Mom cuts her eyes at Ali. "That reminds me—a friend of mine works for a medical practice nearby. They're looking for a new office manager. She could probably get you an interview if you're interested."

"Sounds fascinating," Ali mutters, sliding lower in her chair. She'd blown her bakery interview by asking if peanut allergies were really *that* serious.

"I'm thinking about college," Charlie says, "but I want to help my mom get settled first."

The stern lines on Mom's face melt a little. "That's certainly understandable."

"What about sports?" Dad asks. "Did you play anything in high school? You've got the height for basketball."

"I ran track for a while, but nothing that serious."

"Sports are a huge part of Tess's life," Dad says.

"Dad!" Ali and I exclaim at the same time.

Charlie shifts in his seat.

"He knows that," I say.

Dad ignores me. "I'm just saying, Tess is headed to an extremely competitive college program—probably a professional swimming career and maybe even the Olympics. I don't know if someone who doesn't even play sports can understand that kind of commitment."

I don't know what's redder: my cheeks, Charlie's ears, or the fire coming out of my sister's eyes. "Don't you think that's between them, Dad? Jesus," Ali spits.

"I understand what you're saying, Mr. Cooper," says Charlie. "I'm enjoying learning about the sport, and I completely support Tess's commitment to it. I'm really looking forward to her meet on Saturday."

"I think it's nice for Tess to have something else to focus on for once," Mom says. "Especially right now."

"Mom," I warn.

"The last thing she needs right now is to lose focus," Dad says.

"Could we please not talk about this?" I beg.

Charlie's brows knit together.

My parents seem to have forgotten my presence entirely.

"Her health should be her main focus," Mom says.

"Guys…" Ali tries.

"She's not giving up her dreams on a maybe," Dad grumbles.

"Whose dreams are they, Rob?"

"Could everyone please shut up?" I shout.

Silence settles across the table like a blanket of ice, fragile and deadly. Mom and Dad are locked in a furious staring contest, Ali's pouting as she pushes untouched food around her plate, and poor Charlie looks shell-shocked, like he can't figure out how he wandered into this war zone. Humiliation gnaws at my limbs like frostbite. I push back my chair and storm out of the kitchen.

It's not long before Charlie joins me on the front stoop. I can breathe out here, but when Charlie sits down beside me, his long legs stretched out, my throat seizes.

"That was...weird," he says.

"It's not always like this. My parents are in rare form tonight."

"I get it." Charlie pushes back my hair. His fingers brush my shoulder, and a shiver rushes down my spine. "You okay?"

His eyes are soft with concern, promising not to judge. "I had a doctor's appointment last week," I tell him. "They did this test that was supposed to show how likely I am to have another seizure. We got the results today. My doctor thinks I could have epilepsy." The word feels foreign on my tongue; I want to spit it out.

"Oh."

"I can keep swimming, but I have to take all these dumb precautions for the next six months, just in case. I'll probably suck at Nationals. I could even lose my scholarship." I fight back brimming tears. "This could ruin everything for me."

Charlie leans back on his hands and squints at the sky. I wait for him to tell me there's more to life than making plans. He doesn't say anything at all.

I swipe a gritty palm across my cheek. "I'm a swimmer. I don't know how to be anything else."

"As far as I'm concerned," Charlie says, "the fact that you're a swimmer is the least interesting thing about you."

"Thanks a lot."

"Seriously. It's cool you swim and even cooler you want to go pro, but that's not what makes you special."

A soft, tingling warmth starts in my limbs and climbs up my body, like a slow thaw. "You're smart and dedicated. You're a loyal friend and you're fierce when you need to be. You're funny." Charlie swallows. "It doesn't hurt that you're beautiful."

I nudge his knee with my own. "If I didn't know better, I'd think you have a little crush on me."

"You're all right, I guess."

I laugh.

Charlie pulls me closer and intertwines his arm with mine. "You're definitely a swimmer," he says. "But you're more than that, too."

I lean my head on his shoulder, breathing in the mingling scents of sweat and detergent and the faint, indescribable something that just smells like Charlie. It's the safest I've felt all day.

CHAPTER
THIRTEEN

In the days that follow, Dr. Cappalano's words cycle through my brain on repeat: *We just don't know if you'll have another seizure until you do.* No matter how hard I try to focus on training, my mounting anxiety is a constant distraction. It's like I'm carrying around a ticking time bomb set to *whenever*, and I'm just holding my breath until it detonates.

On Friday, Coach meets me at the end of my lane after practice.

"You feeling okay?" she asks.

"Yeah." I peel off my goggles, run my hands down my face. "I don't know."

"You need to tell me if training is too much."

"It's not that. I'm just off this morning. In my head, I guess."

Coach folds her arms across her clipboard. "You're already going to be swimming with a handicap at Nationals. Mentally, you need to be on your game."

The word *handicap* bows my head like a heavy hand. "I know."

"I expect you to be focused at tomorrow's meet."

I tell her I will be, but doubt has taken root and it festers through the night. Worst-case scenarios play out in my dreams:

demotion to the C Finals at Nationals, humiliating myself in front of the entire swimming community, my scholarship yanked out from under me. Each loss a domino that knocks down the next.

Saturday morning, Dad finds me in the kitchen, making breakfast before the meet. He's dressed in jeans and an Oakwood Academy T-shirt, the softly lined skin around his eyes creased with sleep.

I spread creamy avocado on a slice of toast. "Want some?"

"Coffee first. Always coffee." Dad fills a travel mug to the brim. "You feel ready?"

"I guess."

"Every win counts," he reminds me.

"So does every loss." The food feels like concrete in my throat. "Maybe I shouldn't go."

"To the meet?"

"To Nationals."

Dad lowers his mug. "You're kidding, right?"

"You heard what Coach said about modified training. There's no way I'm going to make the A Finals now."

"C'mon, Tess. One bad test result and you're ready to give up on your dreams?"

"You did."

"That was different," Dad says, his voice tightening. "You can't play ball with a blown knee."

"You can't swim with epilepsy—not really."

"Maybe some people can't, but you're a fighter, kid. You always have been."

I raise my brow, not so sure.

"Even when you first learned how to swim—it was like you belonged in the water, like your body just knew what to do."

"Let's hope it doesn't forget," I say dryly. For the first time in my life, I can't trust my body; it could betray me at any time.

Dad pushes a travel mug across the counter. "We've got this."

I force a smile, thinking if things go south, it won't be "we" gasping for air on the pool deck. It will just be me.

—

The locker room at Mountain Ridge Prep is packed and buzzing with energy. Lockers clang and a din of high-pitched chatter hangs above our heads like a crackling storm cloud.

My teammates have marked a small territory with swim bags and water bottles. Simone is changing into her practice suit. Rachel wears sweatpants and bounces on the balls of her feet like she's about to take the block.

"Hey." Mac wears gym shorts over her practice suit, and she's got a Venti iced coffee in her hand.

"Hey."

Ever since our fight, she's treated me with cool indifference—far worse than the silent treatment, which always eventually ends.

Simone's eyes dart between us. "Are you guys okay?"

Mac nods, avoiding my gaze.

We are not okay. This summer has ripped at our friendship with a serrated blade. I'm not sure we'll ever be the same.

As our team begins to warm up, Coach heads over to the deck ref. I can't hear their conversation, but soon he's clearing out the first lane. The rest of the pool is a can of sardines with swimmers warming up fingers to feet. I slip into the empty lane as a hush settles over the crowd in the stands. A man shouts: "My kid's getting kicked in the face and she gets her own lane?"

"Just ignore him," Davis says. "You have every right to be safe."

I know he's right, but I can't help but feel like I'm pulling into a handicapped parking spot or swiping the largest bathroom. The people in the stands can't see epilepsy; my accommodations just look like special treatment.

Davis guides me through a few familiar drills, finishing with a race pace that leaves my heart throbbing, my body loose, and my mind finally clear. By the time I climb out of the pool, I'm not thinking about the man in the stands or even my EEG results. All I want to do is race.

"Feeling focused?" Coach asks. Her hair is slicked back in a ponytail, and her red team polo is speckled with water.

"Definitely." This meet is the reminder I needed: I belong in the water, and I'm here to win.

Coach taps my hip with her clipboard. "Good girl."

My teammates wait at the end of the pool. "You know this is just a regular meet, right?" Rachel says. "Bringing your own cheer section is kind of overkill."

I follow her gaze to the center of the stands. Charlie and Howie sit in front of my parents, in the very first row. Charlie's holding a giant poster board that reads, DON'T WORRY! NO ONE KNOWS THIS IS FOR YOU! Howie waves when he sees me. The smile that blooms spreads through my chest like a full inhale on a spring day.

There are six heats for my first race, the women's 100-meter free. Rachel and I—grouped with the fastest swimmers—will swim in the sixth heat. As Mac and the other girls in the fourth heat dive into the water, I head over to the blocks. No one complains that I'll race in the first lane; the center is the coveted spot, reserved for the fastest swimmers, and Rachel stands behind the block, rolling out her shoulders. I close my eyes, summoning the feel of the water against my skin. I'm reaching for the touchpad that will seal my time, when a voice interrupts my visualization.

"Don't worry," Davis says. "I'll keep my eyes on you the whole time."

"I'm trying to focus," I snap.

He holds up his hands. "Right. Sorry."

The girls in the fifth heat get into position on the blocks. Now all I can think about is Coach at one end of the pool and Davis on the other, my parents and Charlie in the stands—six pairs of eyes waiting, literally, to see if I sink or swim.

The whistle announces the sixth heat, and I have no choice but to step onto the block.

"Take your marks," the deck ref announces.

I drop low into track stance, but the water isn't clear blue and welcoming. It glows garish green, and the smell of diesel teases my nose. Fear drills my feet to the block, and when the starter buzzes, I freeze.

The other swimmers take air, the splashes jolting me back to reality. I'm only a second too late, but a second is everything.

My heart beats erratically as I crash through the water, and my mind races faster than my body. When my palm finally presses the touchpad, I cut through the surface, my eyes darting to the stands. Charlie and Howie are cheering, but Dad's face is washed in disappointment.

Rachel clings to the side of the pool with a scowl on her face. "What the hell was that?"

My time blinks across the scoreboard: 57:30. Two full seconds slower than I should've been. Rachel creamed me, followed by two other Mountain Ridge girls.

Davis thrusts a towel in my hands. "It's just one event," he says. "Shake it off and move on."

My teammates whisper to one another as I stalk by; pity glances off my shoulders and back like dodgeballs. Mac grabs my arm. "It's one event," she says. "Let it go. Everybody chokes sometimes."

"Not me," I hiss.

Mac's eyes flash, and she drops her hand. "Right. I forgot."

Wrapped in my parka, I sit on my bag, hugging my knees. I can't bear to look up at the stands, where Dad is no doubt mouthing empty words of encouragement: *There's nowhere to go but up.*

This summer has shown me there's always further to fall.

———

My parents are waiting in the parking lot after the meet. The sun hangs low in the sky, casting long afternoon shadows. Dad leans against the van, resting his knee. "There she is!" he announces—too loud, too cheerful.

Mom's smile is plastic. "Great meet, honey."

Around us, families mingle in small clusters. Parents boasting to other parents. Exhausted swimmers reliving their best events. "Can we please get out of here?" I ask.

Dad unlocks the van, and I slump against the dark gray fabric.

"It was just one meet, Tess," Mom tries, buckling her seat belt.

My glare shoots lightning.

"I know the 100 was rough," Dad says, "but you recovered."

"Barely." My time in the 200-meter free was better, which helped me get my head straight for the rest of the meet. But I can't stop thinking about how I choked. The fear came on fast and brutal, a flash forward to what could play out on live TV at Nationals. My phone buzzes.

Charlie: **Sorry we had to leave. Howie had to be somewhere at 2. Was this meet longer than most?**

I'm typing my response when another text comes through.

Charlie: **You were great, btw. If you ran as fast as you swim, I'd be screwed.**

Dad's broad hands clutch and unclutch the steering wheel. "It's those damn modifications," he mutters. "I'm going to have a talk with Higgins."

"You know those modifications are about Tess's safety," Mom says.

The volley starts—back and forth—like I'm not even here.

"Training like this is nothing but a surefire way to kill her swimming career. We have her happiness to consider, too."

"This is not a sore tendon or a broken bone. This is a seizure disorder. Do you even understand what that means?"

"Do you?" I explode. "A seizure disorder is literally the worst possible thing that could happen to me."

"Lower your voice, Tess," Dad says, but I ignore him.

"Let's just say, by some miracle of the universe, I actually make the A Finals at Nationals and sign with Northern Hills. How long do you think I have before they realize I'm a fraud? A year, tops? No school in the country is going to pay for a swimmer that can't actually swim."

"She's right, Rob," Mom says.

Dad grows quiet, like the full implication of an epilepsy diagnosis is finally dawning on him. I slam my hand against the window, so hard my palm comes back red.

I want out I want out I want out.

———

A Google search of swimmers with epilepsy only solidifies my fear—even the Paralympics, the pinnacle competition for elite athletes with physical disabilities, excludes epileptics from qualification. My seizure follows me around like a black dot on my permanent record; the possibility of another affects nearly every aspect of my life. But to everyone else, epilepsy is invisible.

Ali opens my bedroom door, takes in my wet hair and pj's. "It's Saturday night," she says. "Don't you have something better to do?"

Charlie wanted to go out, but I'd told him I was too tired after swimming all day. Mostly I just don't want to talk about the meet, especially with someone who's going to try to make me feel better about it—Ali included. "What do you want?"

"I'm bored. Let's watch a movie?" She flops across my bed and grabs my laptop.

"Hey!" I snatch it back, but not before she gets a good look at my search results.

"The Special Olympics?" she asks.

"The Paralympics. It's different, not that it matters."

Ali raises her brow.

"I was looking into a backup plan." My fingers trace the peeling edges of the Oakwood Academy sticker on my laptop. "You know, just in case."

"I'm guessing the meet didn't go so well?"

So much for not talking about it. I fill her in on the suckage—choking and my fight with Mom and Dad. "If it was up to Mom, I probably would've quit the team already."

"Maybe that wouldn't be such a bad thing," Ali muses.

"You have got to be kidding."

"Hear me out," she says. "For the past three years, your life has been completely consumed by swimming, right? No dates, no real social life. Just swim, school, repeat. Maybe this is a chance to relax a little, be a normal teenager for once."

"I don't want to be normal, Al. I have goals. A plan. Stuff that's way more important to me than parties and boys."

"All I'm saying is change isn't always the worst thing in the world. Sometimes, it can be really good, even if you can't see that yet."

"Oh, really? I didn't realize they teach psychology at waitressing school."

"You're hurting, so I'll let that go. But you don't have to be a bitch." She slides off my bed. "I think I'll watch a movie alone tonight."

I flop back and groan into my pillow. Maybe change is good for some people—maybe it's good for Ali and Charlie. But my skin feels inside out; everything hurts and nothing is working out the way it's supposed to. There is nothing good about that.

CHAPTER
FOURTEEN

Practice is canceled on the Fourth of July, and Dad and I work out at the school where he coaches. By the time we get home, our usually quiet neighborhood bustles with preparations for the annual summer block party.

Mom's icing brownies in the kitchen. I grab a coconut water and plop down at the island. My Instagram feed is full of celebrations, but one image pulls me up short: Rachel and Mac at the shore. Mac's wearing a bikini top she borrowed from me last summer. Suddenly, I'm desperate to get it back.

"You look worn out," Mom says.

I push away my phone. "Dad's a good coach."

He's sneaking a spoonful from the huge bowl of pasta salad he made this morning. Mom shoots him a look.

"I've been thinking," she says. "There may be other college options we haven't considered."

"Like what? Community college?"

"Not necessarily." She sprinkles stars across the frosting. "There are several perfectly good schools within hours of here.

Your grades could get you in anywhere, and I'm sure it's not too late to apply for an academic scholarship."

"Surprise, surprise," Ali says, breezing into the kitchen, her tone cocked like a loaded weapon. "Mom's talking about college. What else is new?"

Taking the opportunity to escape, I slide my phone off the counter and back away before I get caught in the cross fire.

———

Outside, sherbet-colored streaks splash across the blue-gray sky. A din of conversation hovers over the neighborhood like charcoal smoke. Families lounge around tables full of burgers, corn on the cob, and potato salad, and kids dart from yard to yard, gathering glowsticks and dessert. At Charlie's, the lights in the living room window twinkle invitingly, and neighbors mingle on the lawn. He's locked in a very intense arm-wrestling match with Howie, the veins in his neck straining against his skin. He groans as Howie presses his arm to the table, and a girl cheers.

"You make it too easy," Howie says.

Charlie stretches his forearm. "Show-off." He stands up and pulls me in for a hug.

"Tess, right?" Charlie's aunt Denise sits in the grass near the table. She wears cutoff shorts and a flowy peasant top, her hair piled into a swirling bun at the crown of her head. I introduce myself, and then meet Howie's girlfriend, Rosemary.

"C'mon," Charlie says. "I want you to meet my mom." He steers me to the far end of the lawn, where a woman with dark curls plies a miniature version of Charlie with a barely touched burger. "Three more bites if you want to have dessert," she says.

The little boy scrunches his face tight and waves a glowstick like he's trying to cast a burger-blocking spell.

"Mom," Charlie says, "this is Tess."

"Nice to meet you, Mrs. Howard." Three syllables too late, I realize I've stuck my foot in my mouth.

The woman's cheeks tinge pink. "Please, call me Carol."

"Carol," I echo dumbly.

Charlie's little brother darts away. "Max!" his mom calls.

"I'll get him." Charlie takes off after the runaway, who's just disappeared under a table.

"He's so good with his brother," Carol says. "I don't know what I'd do without him these days."

I toy with the loose skin on my elbow, wondering how I'm supposed to respond.

"Howie's been talking about your meet all week. I hear you're quite the swimmer."

"It was sweet of him to come."

"You've been swimming a long time, I guess?"

"Since elementary school."

"When Charlie was little, he tried every sport there was. Did he tell you he used to run track?"

I nod. "I bet he was really fast."

"Like lightning." A small sigh softens her shoulders and the puffy skin around her mouth. "But his dad was his coach and…" She shakes her head. "I'm just so glad he's met someone. The move was really hard on him."

"It was?" I ask, hoping she'll say more. Charlie always seems so easygoing, except for when he talks about his dad.

"I got a brownie!" Max announces as Charlie strides across the lawn, his brother clinging to his back like a baby koala.

"That was supposed to be our secret." Charlie smiles at me. "Do you want to go get some food? It's going fast."

I hesitate, not ready for my conversation with his mom to end. I want to know what keeps Charlie up at night, what he's running away from.

His brow furrows. "Everything okay?"

"Everything's fine," I say. "Let's go eat."

———

Charlie scrapes the last bite of potato salad from his plate and then lies back on my lawn, one hand behind his head and the other on his full belly.

"Finished?" I tease.

"For now," he says, closing his eyes. "Check with me in twenty minutes."

The sky has deepened in color, and some families are already starting to migrate down the street with blankets and lawn chairs, determined to snag prime firework-viewing real estate at the middle school athletic field. I pluck a few blades of grass, roll them between my fingers. There's no bridge into this conversation. If I want to know about Charlie's past, I just have to take the plunge.

"Can I ask you a question?"

"Shoot."

"It's about your dad."

Charlie squints one eye open. "My mom said something, didn't she?"

"Just that the move was hard on you."

"Yeah?"

"You never want to talk about him. I guess I'm just wondering why."

Charlie's hand rests on my knee; his thumb traces a rainbow arc on my skin. "There's nothing to talk about really."

"He clearly hurt you."

"He left my mom for another woman. When Mom said she wanted sole custody, he just gave us away. So, yeah. He hurt me. He hurt all of us. Moving here was supposed to be our fresh start."

"Have you talked to him since?" I ask.

A tight ball forms at Charlie's jawline. "I closed that door. It's not worth opening again."

How can you have a fresh start when you never had an ending? All that talk about not needing a plan—Charlie's so busy running away, he hasn't given any thought to where he's headed.

"Maybe it would help," I try.

"Nah," Charlie says, sitting up. "I don't like to think about the past. I'd rather focus on the good stuff, you know? Hanging out with Howie, my job at the Y." He tucks back my hair, his thumb brushing my cheekbone. "You."

A shiver runs down my spine. I lean closer, feeling Charlie's breath warm against my skin.

"You guys coming to watch the fireworks?" Dad's voice jerks us out of the moment.

My family is headed up the driveway. Mom gives me an apologetic smile. "We just came to get lawn chairs."

"Want to go?" I ask, and Charlie agrees.

"Great," Dad says. "I'll grab extra chairs."

"Dad…"

Ali saves me. "Pretty sure they want to watch the fireworks together, Dad. Alone."

"Right." Dad stares at us for a minute. Charlie tugs on the collar of his T-shirt. "I guess we'll see you guys there."

"Have fun," Mom says.

"We will," I tell her.

"Enjoy the 'fireworks,'" Ali says, putting finger quotes around the word.

Shut up, I mouth, pushing Charlie toward the street.

———

The middle school athletic field looks like a beach in mid-summer; it's covered with blankets and camping chairs. Kids dart between groups, glowing bracelets hanging from their wrists. "Let's go up there," Charlie says, pointing to a narrow spot at the very top of the bleachers. "Best seats in the house are open."

"There's barely room for one person."

"So we'll ask them to scoot over."

We pick our way up the bleachers, like those annoying people who come late to a movie. I apologize to everyone we pass. When we finally make it to the top, Charlie gives a sheepish grin to the people on the bench. "I'm so sorry, but would you guys mind scooting over a little?" He sticks his thumb at me. "She just *had* to sit at the top."

They squish together, creating a small space at the end of the row. Charlie plops down. "Found us a spot."

I squeeze into the narrow space, glaring at him. A loud boom rumbles across the field, and light prickles above the tree line. Then a single golden arrow streaks across the darkness, and the sky breaks open. Golden, green, blue, and red sparkles fill the night, so close I can almost taste the ash.

Charlie's chin turns up; his skin glows red and green. "Do you do this every year?"

"Every year I can remember. Usually Mac comes, too." I don't mean to bring her up—reflex, I guess. Mac's always been a part of my story, and now I'm tripping around the gaping hole she left on the page.

"You miss her, huh?"

I look out at the field, where last summer, Mac and I watched the fireworks from a blanket in the grass. Tan, sticky with sweat, and full of picnic food, we'd had a plan for our lives, a plan that kept us together no matter what. Last summer we could've never imagined all the ways life would betray us. "Yeah," I say, blinking back tears.

Charlie clears his throat. "I thought moving here was the worst thing that could've ever happened. This summer—meeting you—I didn't expect it. But I wouldn't change it either."

It dawns on me if I was still lifeguarding, Charlie and I never would've met. For a second, a whole future opens up in front of me, full of new and different, but not necessarily bad. Like wild-flowers in a vegetable garden, surprising you with their unexpected beauty.

"Me neither," I tell him, winding my fingers through his. We lean back against the fence as the sky explodes—one firework after another, illuminating the entire sky.

CHAPTER
FIFTEEN

"Ugh, why are these kids so needy?" Taro groans, tossing a Drumstick into the waiting hands of a soaking-wet middle schooler.

I snip the plastic wrapper off the top of a blue freeze pop, relishing the chill against my palm. The sun is relentless, the air dry and stiff, and the pool is packed. On the lifeguarding chair, Charlie's got a towel across his shoulders and a line of empty water bottles beside his feet.

"Next in line for cavities and diabetes!" Taro calls out.

Charlie blows the whistle, ending adults-only swim, and the air fills with shrieks of joy. Even the last few kids in line abort mission, darting back to their chairs to dump their change before diving in with their friends.

"Finally," says Taro, climbing onto the stool and picking up his phone.

Familiar voices draw my attention to the pool gates, where Rachel is checking in. Seth is with her, shirtless, a light blue beach towel slung across his broad shoulders and his swim trunks hanging low on his hips.

"I def wouldn't mind getting my sun goddess on," grumbles Taro.

Mac joins them during her break. She spritzes Rachel's back with sunscreen, giggling as Seth does a cannonball that splatters them both. Resentment is a riptide, but above it, truth dawns: Change may have brought me Charlie, but it's taking Mac. And I'm not ready to lose her.

"I'll be right back," I tell Taro.

He gives me a dismissive wave without looking up from his phone.

My heart thrums as I near my teammates, like I'm about to take an uninvited seat at the cool table in the cafeteria, or ask a guy to Sadie Hawkins. Saving my friendship with Mac doesn't feel at all like a sure thing.

Seth sits on the edge of her chair, finger-painting her back with sunscreen.

"Hey," he says as I approach.

Both girls squint up at me. "Can we talk?" I ask Mac.

She looks at Rachel like she's asking permission.

Rachel shrugs. "I'm getting in the water."

"Me too," says Seth. They head to the diving board, cutting right in front of a handful of kids.

"What do you want to talk about?" Mac asks.

"I don't know." I drop onto the empty chair beside her. "I'm just sick of *not* talking."

Mac stares at her toes—unpainted, I observe, and then realize that's a weird thing to notice. Except it's not. At the beginning of the summer, I knew Mac's favorite polish and when she'd bought her last bottle. Now I feel like I don't know her at all. The small space between us yawns like a chasm, too deep and rocky to cross. "It just feels like we're broken. And I want to put us back together, but I don't know how."

"It's my fault," Mac blurts, the quake in her voice a bridge. "I acted like an idiot at Seth's party, and then I lied to you…"

"I don't care about that stuff anymore," I tell her, realizing it's true. Our fracture began well before the summer, when I was so focused on my own future, my own goals, that I wasn't the friend Mac needed me to be. Suddenly, I want to do it all over, because I need her, too—now more than ever. "You're my best friend, Mac. I miss you. I miss us."

Her lip trembles. Then she throws her arms around me. The hug is a welcome cloud of chlorine and coconut sunscreen and the quintessential Mac smell that lingers in my hairbrush and on my second pillow and on the borrowed sweatshirts draped around my room. "I miss you, too," she says.

"Guys, look!" Seth calls, double-bouncing the board and leaping into a front flip that sends a tidal wave to either side of the pool. A couple kids scramble to safety as Rachel claps. "I give it a ten!"

Mac rolls her eyes.

"Do you want to hang out tonight?" I ask, holding my breath in anticipation that Mac already has plans with Rachel or Seth.

"I'd like that," she says.

And I exhale.

—

We grab dinner after practice. Mac picks the place: a brick oven pizzeria serving pillowy homemade dough and enough cheese to make even Dad swoon. We choose a table outside, where the air smells like summer—honeysuckle, freshly mowed grass, and freedom. We talk about our weekends, the picnic and fireworks, Mac's trip to the shore.

"Rachel's parents are keto," she tells me, sinking her teeth into a fat slice of pizza. "I spent the weekend dreaming about your dad's pasta salad."

I laugh, thinking how Charlie would die of starvation in a carb-free environment. "I told Charlie he hadn't really lived until he experienced a Creek Lane block party. I don't think he believed me, but between the fireworks and potato salad, I'd say he's converted."

Mac waggles her brows.

"What?"

"You and Charlie. It's been a few weeks now, right?" She taps my leg with her foot. "I need details."

I take another bite of pizza. "What do you want to know?"

"Oh, I don't know…" Mac taps out questions on her fingers. "Number one, is he a good kisser? Number two, is he a good kisser? Number three—"

"Okay, okay, I get it!" I laugh. My cheeks fill with heat as I think about the brush of Charlie's lips, the pull of his tongue.

"Oh. My. God," Mac says.

"What?"

"You had THE kiss!"

"What kiss?"

"Don't pretend you don't know exactly what I'm talking about," Mac says, pointing her pizza at me. "The sweep-you-off-your-feet-head-in-the-clouds-leaves-you-breathless kiss. Like in the movies. The kiss to beat all kisses. No matter who you kiss next, you'll always compare them to kissing Charlie."

Charlie and I haven't been together that long, and who knows what's going to happen between us. But right now, his is the only mouth I want on mine. "He is pretty perfect," I say, earning a gleeful clap from Mac. The comfort of being here, stuffing our faces and talking about boys, is so sweet it stings a little.

"I've missed this so much," I say. "I can't remember the last time we actually hung out, just the two of us."

Wheels turn in Mac's eyes as her memory ticks backward with mine. The last time we truly spent time together was in the hospital—the morning after everything changed for both of us.

A hard line draws Mac's brows close. "I had a really hard time after…" She doesn't finish the sentence, like even the word *seizure* calls up a memory she can't bear. "No matter how hard I tried, I couldn't forget how scared I was that night. And hanging out with you…"

"What?" I lean forward, almost desperate. Maybe if we name the wedge between us, it will dissolve.

"It reminded me."

I reel. Mac's been trying to escape that night as desperately as I have, but to her, I'm a living, breathing reminder.

She runs her hands through her hair, tugging the ends. "I feel like a selfish asshole. You're the one who lived it, who's still living it."

"That's why you've been spending so much time with Rachel," I breathe.

"Don't get me wrong," Mac says. "She can be a real bitch when she wants to be. But she lets me talk about it. She listens."

"We could've talked about it."

"Could we?" Mac presses gently. "Because that morning, after the party, talking about it seemed impossible."

"You're right." I take a sip of soda, the bite burning at the back of my throat. "I've wanted to forget, too. And that's getting harder and harder to do."

"But you're swimming again," Mac says. "And with all that safety stuff you're doing, it seems like things are almost back to normal for you."

"It's actually been the opposite." I tell her about my EEG

results, how every day since has felt like walking on a frozen lake, like at any moment, the ice could crack and I'll slip under.

"Coach asked tonight if I'm ready to work on pace again," I tell her. "And I just gave her some lame excuse to put it off." I crunch ice cubes between my teeth. "I keep waiting to not be afraid anymore, but it's only getting worse."

"What about Nationals?" Mac asks.

"I mean, I'll have to swim in the outside lane; Coach will be constantly hovering. I know that stuff is supposed to keep me safe, but it also just reminds me, you know? Every time I get in the water, I'm risking my life. And for what? I haven't signed my scholarship yet. They'd have every right to rescind it if I can't perform. And from what I can tell, there's only a handful of professional swimmers with epilepsy."

"So?" Mac says.

I blink. "So what?"

"So who says you can't be one of them? Who cares if there aren't many swimmers with epilepsy? Maybe you can be one of the first."

"It's not that easy, Mac."

She laughs. "Since when have you ever done anything the easy way?"

We stay at the pizzeria until our stomachs are empty again, and then we stop at Sprinkles on our way back to Mac's house. We watch a rom-com on her bedroom floor and it's almost like old times—before my seizure, before the summer changed us. Our friendship has sore spots, chipped edges, and a few scars that won't ever go away. It's fragile and imperfect, but real.

Later, as I crawl into bed, my mind picks up Mac's words like smooth stones, rolling them back and forth until they shine. What if I swam anyway? Not because I never had a seizure, but because I did. What if I don't let it take swimming away?

CHAPTER
SIXTEEN

Curled up on Charlie's couch, with *Star Wars* playing in the background, I scroll through my phone, taking a closer look at the handful of epileptic swimmers I'd dug up. One woman blogs about how long it took her to conquer her fear; she stopped competing altogether. A few articles feature a guy who made it all the way to Olympic Trials. I want a playbook to get me from point A to point B, but none of these stories are the same. It's encouraging and terrifying all at the same time.

"Hey, are you even watching?" Charlie asks, bumping my arm with his elbow.

"Yeah," I lie, lowering my phone.

"Pop quiz: Who's Obi-Wan Kenobi?"

"Um. Is that the green guy?"

"No!" Charlie snatches my phone in mock exasperation. "No more scrolling."

"Hey!" I protest, scrambling over him to rescue my phone. "You're lucky you're cute, you know that?"

Charlie smirks, his dimple winking. "You think I'm cute?"

"Yeah, when you're not geeking out over aliens."

"In that case—" He turns off the movie, his body pressing closer to mine.

"You mean, you'd pass on an afternoon of *Star Wars* for me?" I tease.

"You have no idea."

"Even the little green guy?"

Charlie's eyes widen. "For the last time, his name is—"

I stop his mouth with mine.

It's not long until Charlie's phone alarm interrupts us. He groans as our bodies untangle. "I have to go to work," he says, turning off the alarm.

"I thought you were off today."

"The Y," he reminds me. "Swim class."

"Right." I flop backward on the couch, not ready for one of my few free afternoons with Charlie to end.

He hovers over me. "Come with me?"

"Really?"

"It'll be fun," he says, tugging me to my feet. "Cute kids, cute boyfriend…"

The word slips out so naturally, but Charlie's ears suddenly ignite and his eyes can't seem to find focus. "I mean, if you want to…"

"I'd love to," I say.

———

Howie's working at the front desk when we arrive at the YMCA. "Sunshine!" he says, coming around the check-in stand to give me a hug.

"I see where I rank now," Charlie says.

"Hey there, Charlie." A man steps out of the office near the lobby. He's tall, with ebony skin and a perfect fade. "We've got a new family joining the class today. Just wanted to give you a heads-up."

"Sure thing." Charlie gestures to me. "This is Tess. Is it cool if she helps out today? She's a lifeguard, too."

"Used to be," I correct him. "I was just going to watch the class."

"Ian," the man says, holding out his hand.

"She's the best swimmer in the whole country, Sports Guy," Howie chimes in.

Ian chuckles. "I'm the athletic director, but I like the nickname. And with that kind of endorsement from Howie, how can I say no?"

Charlie leads me to the pool, where I help him set out noodles and kickboards. Soon families join us on the deck, parents with excited kids that hurry to choose their favorite color kickboard before splashing down the stairs into the shallow end. I sit on the side of the pool, my bare feet trailing circles in the water as Charlie guides the pairs through their lesson.

"That's my friend Tess," he tells the kids. "Can you kick so hard you splash her?"

A collective giggle rises from the water as small legs strain to sprinkle me.

The pool door opens and Ian steps through, a mom and daughter close behind him. The little girl takes one look at the pool and clings to her mom's leg, burying her face in the fabric of her shorts. Charlie stands in the middle of the pool, helping parents tug their kids from one side to the other on kickboards.

The mom is obviously flustered and Charlie is in no position to leave the rest of the class. So I grab a rubber ducky from the bucket of toys at the side of the pool and head over to meet them. "Hi," I say, kneeling down so I'm face-to-face with the little girl. "I'm Tess. This is my rubber ducky."

The little girl unglues her face from her mom's shorts and peers curiously at the duck.

"Do you want to hold it?" I ask.

She reaches for the toy.

"He loves the water," I tell her. "Do you want to see him swim?"

She hesitates, her eyes trailing to the pool then back to the duck. When I offer her my hand, she takes it.

"May I?" I ask her mom.

Relief spreads across the woman's face. "Please," she says.

Thank you, Ian mouths.

I lead the little girl to the pool stairs where she sits down beside me. I show her how the duck floats and I bring it back to her whenever the water carries it too far. Eventually, she puts her tiny feet on the stair beside mine. By the end of class, I'm able to trickle a handful of water down her leg.

When class is over and the parents have herded their children into the locker rooms, Charlie swims over to me. "You're hired," he says, his fingers circling my ankles. "You're now my official assistant."

"I don't know. 'Supervisor' has a better ring to it." I reach to splash him, but he grabs my hand, tugging me forward. "I'm not wearing a—" It's too late. I'm in the water, my shorts and T-shirt soaked through, Charlie's arms wrapped around my waist.

"You're pretty great, you know that?"

I smile up at him. "I'm a catch."

A loud cough interrupts us. A middle-aged woman in a swim skirt stands in the locker room door with her hand on her hip. "Water aerobics is starting in five minutes," she snaps. "Are you the teacher?"

"Definitely not," Charlie says as we hurriedly clamber out of the pool.

Ian greets us in the lobby. "Thanks for your help today, Tess. You were great with that little girl."

"She just needed a slow introduction," I say.

Ian smiles. "Well, whatever you did, that mom really appreciated you. If being the best swimmer in the country doesn't work out, you can always come work at the Y."

"Assistant," Charlie coughs.

I give him a sweet smile. "Supervisor."

———

Heat smacks me in the face Friday morning when I let Huck out. We take a short walk around the neighborhood, but I'm sweating when we get home, and my poor dog is panting like he just ran five miles.

Mom nurses a cup of coffee in the kitchen. "You didn't go for a jog, did you?"

"We literally walked two blocks," I tell her, as Huck scrambles for his water. "It's a thousand degrees outside."

"There's a heat advisory," Mom warns. "Make sure you stay hydrated."

The locker room is quiet when I arrive for practice. My teammates cast nervous glances at each other; even Rachel seems tense as she silently changes into her practice suit.

"What's going on?" I ask Mac.

"Underwaters," she tells me. "Coach already has the tarp out."

My chest seizes at the thought of an underwater workout. The last time I raced underwater, I wound up in the ER.

"I'm sure you don't have to do it," Mac says. "Coach will understand."

Davis meets me outside the locker room. "I was supposed to text you last night," he explains. "Coach wants you to take the morning off." Relief wrings me out like a sponge, followed almost immediately by searing shame. One month until Nationals, and I can't even practice with my team.

"I can handle it," I say, hating the uncertainty in my voice.

Davis opens his mouth to respond, but Coach cuts him off.

"Absolutely not." She's just come from her office, her clipboard in hand. "Davis, I thought you were going to let her know."

He gives an apologetic shrug. "I forgot."

Coach scans the pool, where a few people have started warming up. She checks her watch. "I don't have time to put together a new plan. Hit the gym. Davis will come check on you in a bit."

My skin crawls as I map out a workout and select the heaviest weights I can manage, desperate to prove I'm just as strong and capable as I was before my seizure. Even as sweat gathers at my hairline, my body longs for something more, something faster, something to drown out the swirling thoughts of failure and defeat that pound against my skull. I need to run.

Excited, nervous voices trickle from the pool into the hallway as my teammates gear up for underwaters. I break into a jog and push through the doors into the broiling sunlight.

An inner voice nags about the heat advisory. But I am so sick of being careful and safe. Soon that voice is silenced by the pounding of my feet against the pavement and the rhythmic inhale, exhale of my lungs.

The grass along the sidewalk is parched and brown, and the white concrete blurs my vision. A mile or so in, and my skin is burning, my back drenched with sweat. As my legs begin to stretch farther, faster, and my arms pump back and forth, I finally start to feel like myself again. Fierce, focused, and unstoppable.

By the time I reach my neighborhood, my throat is so dry it burns, and my chest heaves with the effort to breathe. I slow to a walk near my house and try to control my breath. It comes in like a wheeze, and my knees suddenly feel like water. The world around me spins; black pinpoints speckle the light. I try to call for my mom, but the word is a guttural cry, an escape of air from a collapsing diaphragm, and somewhere, far away, I feel myself fall.

CHAPTER
SEVENTEEN

Something moist and scratchy tickles the side of my face. I blink my eyes open, but the light is blinding, and pain pulses in my ears. When I try to speak, it comes out like a groan; my spit tastes like metal.

"Try not to move," a gentle voice says. "They're on their way."

I recognize the figure kneeling beside me, the little dog she scoops into her arms. Why can't I find her name?

Sirens wail in the distance, growing closer.

"Tess!" My mom's voice calls from somewhere far away. A dog barks, loud and frantic. "Oh my God, Tess!" The sirens grow louder, and Mom's cool hands sting my skin. She lifts my head into her lap and wipes something off my cheek. Footsteps running, and then Ali's there, too.

"Is she breathing?" she asks, and then, "Oh my God," over and over again.

The air smells like diesel, and an engine hums nearby. The rough brush of thick fabric, and then another voice says my name. "Tess?" Loud, like a teacher in class. "Tess, can you hear me?"

"Here," I'm supposed to say, but my mouth can't find the word.

I force a nod, and the movement jostles my brain, like it's already floating in formaldehyde, and suddenly I'm going to throw up.

Spasms seize my stomach and hot bile fills my mouth. Someone rubs my back as clear liquid streaked with red spills onto the concrete. Am I bleeding? Why am I bleeding?

Mom gently lowers my head to the pavement. Firm hands slide something hard beneath me and then I'm lifted.

The air smells like rubber. Something pricks my arm, stings. Metal doors slam. The engine growls.

Inhale, exhale. Reach, pull.

I swim into the darkness.

———

When I next break the surface, a woman in blue scrubs hovers over me, busily attaching tubes and wires.

I struggle to make sense of where I am.

The gray cabinets. The muted pastel curtain. And the smell. Bleach, sweat, and puke.

"Mom?" My cracked lips taste like blood.

Her face swims into view. "I'm here, honey," she says, rushing to the bedside. "Ali's here, too. Daddy's on his way."

Ali squeezes my trembling leg. "She's still shaking," she says. "Why is she shaking?"

"How are you feeling, Tess?" asks the woman in scrubs.

She's too loud. I can taste her loudness.

"My head," I groan.

"I'll get the doctor to put in an order for pain medicine."

"It's going to be okay," Mom murmurs. But my body is the aftermath of an earthquake, everything split into pieces. I close my eyes and slip away.

———

The pain is quieter when I next wake up, but my tongue is thick and the side of my face aches.

Mom's dozing in the corner—I wonder what time it is.

"Nice to see you, kid," Dad says, leaning over my bed.

Mom jerks awake, and, seeing my eyes open, scrambles out of the chair. "Hi, honey." Her eyes and voice are bleary with sleep, but her relief reaches out to me. "How are you feeling?"

"A little better." My voice cracks, like I haven't had water in days. The sticky squares on my chest itch underneath my gown, and the skin above my cheek feels stretched too tight. I touch the sore spot with tentative fingers, hissing as they land on what feels like skin scraped raw. "What happened?"

"You had another seizure, honey," Mom says. "A bad one. A neighbor saw it happen."

Denise's gentle voice whispers at the back of my mind; Pickles licks my cheek. I smell diesel, hear my mom's scream. Chills prickle my skin.

"My cheek..."

My parents exchange a look across the bed. Dad clears his throat. "You went down pretty hard."

"They called Dr. Cappalano," Mom says. "She wants us to come in first thing Monday."

I try out the truth on my tongue, rolling it against the roof of my mouth.

Epilepsy.

The word knocks against my teeth, scrapes my stiff and swollen tongue.

"What about training?" I need Dad to tell me there's a way out of this, some kind of loophole that gets me back in the water, headed to Northern Hills.

His jaw flexes, his silence loud and clear. Tears sizzle across the raw skin on my cheek. My swimming career ended the moment my face hit the pavement.

—

It's dark when we get home. Dad and Ali help me out of the car and up the stairs as Mom and Huck trail behind.

In the bathroom, my mom and sister help me out of my stiff and smelly clothes, lingering even as I shower. Their hushed whispers evaporate like steam.

Mom helps me towel off and slip on clean pj's. She guides me to my bed, where Ali's already pulled back the covers.

"I don't think you should be alone tonight," Mom says. "Want me to stay?"

"I can," Ali offers.

Mom hesitates.

"You've been up all night, Mom," Ali says. "I've got this. Go get some sleep."

Mom rubs the back of her neck. Deep circles darken the skin under her eyes. "You'll come get me if…anything happens?"

Fear drums in my chest, like the next beat could be my last. "Nothing's going to happen," Ali says, kicking off her flip-flops and sliding under the covers.

Mom's cool hand pushes back my hair; her dry lips press against my skin. "I'm so glad you're here," she says to Ali, squeezing my sister's arm.

"Me too."

Dad taps on the door. He's freshly showered, his damp hair sticking up slightly. Huck brushes past him, leaps onto my bed, and curls into a snuffling ball across my feet.

"Does anybody need anything?" Dad asks. "I could sleep on the floor."

Mom touches his shoulder on her way out. "I'm going to take a shower."

"We're okay," Ali says. "Right?"

"Yeah," I lie.

Dad tugs the comforter up to our shoulders, patting down the edges, like we're little girls again. "Keep an eye on 'em for me," he says, patting Huck's head.

When I was little, I'd crawl into bed with my sister anytime it stormed. She'd grumble but let me snuggle in beside her. The whisper of her warm breath against my hair would eventually lull me back to sleep. In the morning, the storm would be over, the sky clear.

Tonight, a single truth keeps my mind wide awake: this storm isn't going to pass.

CHAPTER
EIGHTEEN

In the morning, Ali's side of the bed is cold, but a mug of coffee waits on the bedside table. I find my mom and sister tucked underneath a blanket on the couch, Huck sprawled on the carpet at their feet.

"How do you feel this morning?" Mom asks. She scoots to the far end of the couch, creating a pocket-sized space for me to climb into.

"Like a trash truck backed over me. Twice."

Ali spreads the blanket across my lap. "Thanks for the coffee," I say, and she kisses my unmarred cheek.

Huck lays his head on my lap, and I stroke the fur between his watery eyes. An awkward silence hangs in the air, smelling slightly sour, like sweat and worry.

Mom takes a sip of her coffee, clears her throat. "I called Coach Higgins. Told her you won't be at practice for a while."

The old me would've argued. But this strange new reality is as undeniable as the throbbing in my temples and the stinging of my cheek. The only thing I want right now is a handful of Advil and a day in bed. "Thanks," I say.

Mom pats my knee. "Want some breakfast? I can make eggs."

"Sure."

Ali seconds the request. "More coffee, too, please?"

Pans clang in the kitchen as Mom finds the skillet.

"Does it feel like the worst hangover in the world?" Ali asks.

"Pretty much."

Huck's suddenly alert, his nose pointing at the living room door. There's a knock, hesitant, and then louder.

Ali peers through the peephole as Mom sticks her head in the living room, the spatula in her hand smeared wet and yellow. "Who is it?" she asks.

"Charlie," Ali says.

Mom's fingers fly to her mouth. "I forgot!"

I stare at her.

"He came to the hospital," she says. "Denise and his cousin, too. They wanted to make sure you were okay."

"Mom!" Ali gapes. "That's kind of a big thing to forget!"

Mom waves the spatula. "At least I remembered now. Anyway, you were sleeping, so Dad thanked them and sent them away." The wet-dog smell of burning eggs trickles into the room, and she rushes to the rescue.

My body complains as I climb off the couch, the blanket trailing after me. Charlie's face is stricken; his eyes widen as he takes in the raw skin on my cheek. "I didn't know if you were..."

I press my face against his chest, feel his shuddering exhale. His arms enclose me until nothing exists but the steady beating of our hearts and the reach and pull of our lungs.

—

For the third time in two months, Mom and I sit in the stiff-backed chairs in Dr. Cappalano's office, waiting anxiously for her to make an appearance. I hate that I recognize the bleach-burned smell of this place, that the too-friendly receptionist with eighties bangs knew me when I walked in the door.

Dr. Cappalano steps into the room. "Good morning," she says, settling onto her swivel stool and opening her laptop. Her dark brown eyes skim the raw spot on my cheek that has just begun to crust over. "I see you took a fall."

I nod, and she types something. *FALL RISK*, probably. Like even walking isn't safe anymore.

"How are you feeling this morning?"

"Sore," I tell her. "And I bit my tongue."

"Let's see?" She briefly assesses the black ring around pink flesh—the perfect imprint of clenched teeth.

"The ER doctor told us it was just surface damage," Mom says.

"Looks that way." Dr. Cappalano's fingers fly across the keyboard. *BITER.* "Your bloodwork shows you were quite dehydrated," she says. "I understand you went for a pretty long run."

"In a heat advisory." The sharp edge in Mom's tone cuts me.

Dr. Cappalano types something else. I wonder what the doctor-y word is for *stupid*. Her fingers pause above the keys. "Dehydration can be a huge trigger, as can sleep deprivation, and stress. Going forward, you'll really need to make a concentrated effort to take care of your body—eat right, stay hydrated, and get enough sleep."

"What about swimming?" Mom asks. "Tess has been training— with the precautions you suggested, of course."

Dr. Cappalano skims her screen. "Now that we have more information, I'm going to start Tess on medication. Once she's feeling better, I don't see why she couldn't get back to training, provided she starts slow and continues to take all the safety measures we discussed."

"I'm supposed to race at a national meet in August," I say.

Dr. Cappalano stops typing. "Sometimes, people with epilepsy have to readjust their goals. That doesn't mean they can't live very happy and fulfilling lives. I have patients who compete in sports, go to college, graduate, and get jobs they love. You have a whole life ahead of you, Tess. It just might look a little different than you thought it would."

Red crescents bloom across my palms.

"Now, let's talk medication," the doctor says. "We'll need to try different doses, and we may need to try different types or combinations of medication. The goal is no seizures and no side effects."

"Side effects?" I echo.

Dr. Cappalano types as she talks, her fingers flying across the keys. "Sometimes people have issues with word retrieval, headaches, things like that. It may take some time for your body to adjust."

For the next five minutes, Mom and I learn about various types of seizure medication and their associated side effects. It feels a little like watching one of those commercials on TV: *One pill will cure your acid reflux. You may experience headache, erectile dysfunction, broken bones, eye explosion, or death by paralysis. Call your doctor if you can manage to get to the phone.*

Then we run through the neurological exam that, at this point, I could do on my own. Dr. Cappalano assesses my cheek, her cold hand tilting my head in different directions. "You're lucky it's just a bad scrape," she says. "Running during that kind of heat, it could've been a lot worse."

"*Lucky* isn't exactly the word I'd use."

Dr. Cappalano scribbles something on a Post-it note. "You might feel alone now, but you're part of a huge community, Tess. So many people, just like you, are dealing with the same challenges and thriving. It might help to meet a few of them." She presses the note into my hand. "Tuesday nights at seven."

I glance at the Post-it. An address. "Thanks," I mutter, shoving it in my pocket.

"You're going to get through this," Dr. Cappalano says. "It's hard, but it's not hopeless."

Easy for her to say. As far as I can tell, there's no plan B that still involves swimming. This summer's U-turn has taken me somewhere dark and ugly—a dead end with nowhere else to go.

——

We pick up my prescription on the way home from the doctor's office and order takeout from the Chinese restaurant next door to the pharmacy. My family eats dinner in the living room—Dad in his recliner, Mom and Ali on the couch, me on the floor. Huck sits nearby, his eyes glued to my plate. We're all tired, all stretched beyond our limits, and no one's pretending it's any other way. We're just us, messy with mouths full and sauce on our fingers. I eat like it's the first time I've tasted food. I eat like it's my last meal.

We watch cop show reruns until it's dark outside; Dad's fallen asleep, his empty plate balanced on his belly. Mom turns off the TV and heads into the kitchen, returning with the orange prescription bottle.

My stomach churns as I skim the instructions, zeroing in on the pharmacist's warnings. *May cause drowsiness and/or dizziness. Don't drive a car or operate heavy machinery until you know how this medication affects you. Do not take while pregnant.* I pull my phone out of my pocket to look up the full list of side effects: dizziness, lack of coordination, fever, chills, anxiety, aggression, risk of suicide.

"Risk of suicide?" I exclaim. "Why would Dr. Cappalano put me on something that might make me want to kill myself? Have you seen this list?"

Dad flinches awake. "What? Who's dying?"

"No one," Mom tells him.

"They have to say all of that stuff," says Ali. "Like if even one person felt remotely depressed while they were testing the meds,

they have to add it to the list of things the meds might 'cause.'"
She puts air quotes around the word *cause*. "Like how ibuprofen
says it can cause stomach ulcers."

"It can," I tell her.

Her eyes widen. "Oh."

"All anti-seizure medication can increase anxiety and depres-
sion," Mom says. Her voice carries a cool, scientific undertone as she
recites Dr. Cappalano's words. "Slowly increasing your dose should
minimize side effects. And if it gets bad, she'll switch you to something else. The goal is no seizures and no side effects, remember?"

I toss my phone on the floor. "She can't switch my meds if I'm
already dead."

"What kind of medication did this doctor put her on?" Dad asks.

Mom presses her fingers against her temples. "People take
these meds every day. We'll watch you closely, Tess, and if your
mood changes at all, we'll call the doctor immediately."

The bottle blurs into an orange blob in my hand. I thumb away
tears. "I hate this so much."

"Me too," says Ali.

"Me too," adds Dad.

"We all hate this, Tess," Mom says. "We'll get through it together."

Later, in my room, I finally make the phone call I've been
dreading. Even though I practiced what to say, when Coach picks
up, words fail me.

"Cooper? Cooper, you there?"

"I'm here."

"Is everything okay?"

"I—I'm calling to say I'm not coming back."

"Your mom told me. Sounds like you're starting some meds,
though, and then—"

"I mean ever."

Coach is silent for a minute. When she speaks, her tone stings like salt in the raw spot on my cheek. "You're quitting?"

"I think it's the best thing...for everyone." Coach should be relieved—no more worrying about the liability of a swimmer with epilepsy. She'll be glad to trim the fat. Dead weight and all that.

"You've put in so much time," she protests. "I know it hasn't been easy or all that fun, but you've shown so much heart. I understand if Nationals is too much this year, but quitting altogether..."

Sometimes, people with epilepsy have to readjust their goals, Dr. Cappalano had said. But there isn't an as-good-as situation here. I don't want almost-but. I squeeze my eyes closed, pressing my fingers into the lids until stars ignite the darkness.

"What about Northern Hills?" Coach pushes. "You're willing to give up your scholarship?"

"I guess, yeah."

"You guess?"

Coach doesn't know what it's like to wake up on the hot concrete, staring up into the faces of strangers, not knowing where you are or what happened, only that you need help, and that for the first time in your whole life, you can't help yourself. You're completely and utterly vulnerable. It's the worst feeling in the world.

"You don't understand," I say, surprised by the bite in my tone.

"You're right," Coach says, resigned. "I can't understand. If you're really sure..."

"I'm sure," I say, and I mean it. So why does everything inside me hurt when I say it out loud?

Coach sighs. "Then I'll respect your decision. But we'll miss you, Tess."

She ends the call, and I flop on my bed, waiting for relief that never comes.

CHAPTER
NINETEEN

"Are you sure you're up to this?" Ali asks when we pull into the pool parking lot a few days later. "Like Mom said, there's no reason to rush back to work if you're not ready."

I'm not ready—not for seeing my teammates, not for what my life will look like without swimming. But work I can handle. "I'll be fine. I'll call you if I start feeling bad."

"Promise?"

"Promise."

With Taro left in charge of the Sugar Shack, bags of cookies mingle with chips, and the freeze pops, painstakingly organized, are mixed up like a dropped box of crayons. I spend the morning reorganizing everything, my mind relaxing as I work. If only life was this easy to straighten out—the blue freeze pops go here, the orange ones over there. But there are too many scattered pieces, and it's too hard to see how they all fit together.

Charlie keeps glancing over from his spot near the shallow end, so unfocused Mac has to shut down a splash war happening right in front of him. "Your boyfriend can't keep his eyes off you," she says, lounging in the Sugar Shack on her break. "It'd be cute if it wasn't a life-or-death situation."

"Pretty sure he's waiting for me to keel over," I say. Like my parents and sister, Charlie's been on high alert since I came home from the hospital.

Mac winces. She'd come over as soon as she heard, spent the night and even skipped practice so we could spend the morning binge-watching *Friends* over donut holes and iced coffee. "He's just worried," she says. "We all are."

"That's the problem. Everyone's worry makes it impossible to feel normal."

Mac glances past me. "Incoming," she says.

Rachel's just arrived. She pauses at the Sugar Shack, a designer swim bag slung over one shoulder. "You're alive," she says bluntly, her eyes flitting over the nasty yellow bruise on my cheek.

I steel myself for what I know is coming next.

"I can't believe you quit the team."

"Yep."

Rachel folds her thin arms across her white bikini top. "Well, that's dumb."

"Rach!" Mac reprimands. "She had a seizure!"

"I guess. But remember when Lily swam with pneumonia? And when Amal made it half a season with a torn rotator cuff? It's not like you're having seizures all the time."

I really shouldn't expect anything less than insensitivity from Rachel, but this feels like telling a blind person they're not trying hard enough to see.

"We're this close to Nationals," Rachel says, holding up two fingers. "I just don't get how you can walk away. What if—"

Charlie interrupts her, leaning over the counter, his hair stiff with sweat and chlorine. "Do you have any Gatorade back there? I'm dying."

"I'll check." I head to the fridge, grateful for the opportunity to escape Rachel's line of questioning. My entire life crashed into the pavement when I fell, shattered on the hot asphalt as I seized. Rachel's walking on broken glass.

"Hey, do you guys have plans Saturday night?" Mac asks.

Charlie and I exchange a glance. "No," I tell her.

"The carnival's in town. We should all go!"

"Gross," Rachel says.

Mac scowls at her. "The flying chairs, bumper cars, fried Oreos—what's not to love?"

I laugh. Mac's a carnival ride queen—the only person I know who's taken on the Tower of Terror three times in a row and lived to brag about it.

"You had me at *fried*," Charlie says.

Rachel huffs. "Fine."

I hesitate. Rachel and Seth are the last people I want to hang out with. But I meant what I said to Mac: if she comes with Rachel now, then that's how I'll take her.

"You'll ride the Gravitron with me?"

Mac snorts. "Duh."

—

"Where are we meeting them?" Charlie nearly shouts. I can still barely hear him above the mechanical twang of carnival music, punctuated by joyful screams as the flying chairs swing over our heads.

I glance at my phone. "By the Ferris wheel."

Charlie leads the way through crowds near giddy with excitement as palpable as his fingers looped through mine. "I smell Oreos," he says, swerving toward a food truck.

"Already?"

Charlie tosses me a look of feigned confusion. "It's like we've never met."

The carnival's glow casts a wide net, and as we wait in the jostling concession line, an unfamiliar sense of claustrophobia tightens around my shoulders. I grip Charlie's hand, and he kisses the top of my head. "You good?"

"Yeah," I assure him, but not before I catch a glimpse of concern in his eyes—this is the first time Charlie and I have been out since my seizure. He's worried, too.

We spot Mac and the others waiting by the Ferris wheel. "Finally," Mac says. "I'm being outvoted. We should definitely ride the Drop Tower first, right?"

"That one?" Charlie casts a dubious glance to the nearby ride where people scream in anticipation at the top and then free-fall toward the ground. "I'm pretty deep into this Oreo right now, so..."

"Dude," Mac grumbles. "Didn't anybody ever teach you: ride first, food second?"

Seth weaves his arm around Mac's waist, nuzzles her ear. "C'mon, babe. Let's skip the barfy ones and hit the Ferris wheel. I want to show you the view from the top."

Rachel makes a gagging sound. "Sorry—it's just that you two make me want to vomit. I vote for the bumper cars."

I stifle a smile, thinking of all the children who will head home with whiplash with Rachel behind the wheel.

"Want a partner?" Amal asks.

Rachel rolls her eyes. "Sure."

They peel away from the group, with Lily and Simone tripping after them. Mac casts an apologetic glance as Seth tugs her toward the Ferris wheel. "Gravitron's next. You and me, right?" she calls.

I smile and wave as she disappears into the crowd. As much

as I want to enjoy myself tonight, my senses reach out like search-lights, illuminating every twitch in my skin, every buzz near my ear, as though each sensation might harken another seizure. Though I know I'd be safe with Charlie, I can't help but wonder how many others would watch in morbid curiosity as I writhed on the dusty ground.

"Guess it's just us," Charlie says, popping his last bite of Oreo into his mouth. "Want me to win you a bear or something?" His eyes track the game tents, where a doe-eyed girl coos over her date's pathetic effort at hitting the row of rigged bottles with a ping-pong ball. "On second thought, will you win me a bear?"

Charlie's humor soothes me, but only for a minute, and he can tell. "What's wrong?"

"Truth?"

"Duh."

"I'm a little anxious. I thought I'd be fine tonight, but this…" I gesture to the sensory explosion around us—the warm glow of lights seems blinding and the cheerful music jars. "It's just a lot."

"Want to bail?"

"I feel bad," I admit. "We just got here, and you haven't even had funnel cake."

Charlie shrugs. "I'm here for you. If you want to go, let's go."

My eyes skirt toward the Ferris wheel.

"She'll understand," Charlie says, reading my mind.

"Okay—let's go."

My chest releases as soon as we reach the fairground parking lot. In the Jeep, Charlie cues up Steve Miller Band, and the low croon of music fills the space between us. His fingers find mine, and he jiggles my wrist encouragingly. "Want to talk about it?"

"Not really." I stare out the window as haggard parents load sticky-faced kids into minivans, heading back to their normal lives, most of which are seizure-free. At the beginning of the summer, my biggest problem was how to pay for my new racing suit; now everything hurts, everything's broken, and nothing fits together the way it's supposed to. "I don't know how to explain."

"Try."

I hug my arms around myself, nails digging into skin. "All I want is to feel normal again, but instead I'm a little afraid and a little sad all the time."

Charlie sighs. "Maybe it would help if you tried focusing on the positive."

I grit my teeth. He sounds worse than Mom, who's been trying (and failing) all week to come up with a bright side to the worst news I've ever received. "It's not that easy."

"Sure it is," Charlie says. "I mean, you're alive, right? Isn't that what matters?"

"I guess."

"You guess?"

"I mean, yes," I tell him. "Of course, that's what's important. But my life as I've always known it is over now. I just feel…lost."

Charlie runs his thumb across my knuckles. "You have me."

I stare at his profile, the sharp slope of his nose, his soft, full lips. The way his fingers, likely unconsciously, tap out the music's undercurrent against the steering wheel, and I want that to be enough.

"Everyone goes through stuff, you know?" Charlie continues. "But eventually they get over it, and they move on. I know it hurts now, but with enough time, you'll move on from this, too."

My gut tightens and I yank my hand away. "You mean like you've gotten over your dad?"

"That's different." Charlie's voice drops low, a warning signal I plow right past.

"You don't take his calls; you don't ever talk about him. He hurt you, badly, and it's not like you're dealing with it."

Charlie works his jaw; his fingers tighten around the steering wheel. "That's none of your business—"

"You've been running since the day you got here. Who are you to tell me I'll just move on?"

"He's my dad, Tess. Swimming—which you quit, by the way—is just a stupid sport."

"Stupid?" I explode. "Swimming is who I am! And if you don't understand that, you don't understand me."

Charlie stares at me, his face half hidden in shadow. "Maybe you're right." The note of resignation in his voice nearly breaks my heart. "Maybe I don't."

We barely talk the rest of the way home. When we pull into my driveway, Charlie turns to look at me. "What now?" he asks.

I want to scoot closer to him; I want to trail my fingers down his cheek. But not every hurt can be healed by Froyo in the park and kisses on the swings. I want to let Charlie into my pain; I want to walk with him through his. But the path is treacherous and unfamiliar, and I'm too afraid.

"I think we should break up." The words hang in the air, just past my lips, too far to take back.

Charlie looks stung. "Is that really what you want?"

I force a nod.

He shifts his weight toward the window, his broad shoulder driving space between us. "Fine."

Tears sting my eyes as I climb out of the Jeep. I've barely shut the door when Charlie backs away.

CHAPTER
TWENTY

My pillow smells musty, like unwashed hair. I flip it over and fold it in half, to better see my laptop screen. Over the last week, despite multiple visits from Mac and two pans of Ali's M&M-loaded "breakup brownies," I've lived in a constant haze of heartache without even practice to distract me. Seeing Charlie at work only makes everything worse, and now a double dose of the chalky seizure meds meant to make me "better" have left me nauseous, with a constant headache, subsisting on a steady diet of saltines and Netflix. I'm now on to *Grey's Anatomy*, all the way back to when Meredith first meets Derek.

There's a knock on my door—probably Mom, trying to bribe me out of bed again. Like a sandwich and a shower will put my life back together. She even brought me two new books yesterday, the covers tempting me with their shine. Normally, I'd devour them in the small gaps of time between work and practice. Now, they top my summer reading stack, which I've barely touched. Not that it matters anymore. Without my scholarship to Northern Hills, I'm headed to community college, regardless of grades.

"I'm not hungry," I call, beating Mom to the punch. My windows are gray, with scattered raindrops—another perfect day to stay in bed. I pull my comforter higher on my shoulder. "Please go away."

The door opens.

"I said go—"

"Enough is enough," Dad says, walking over to my bed and closing my laptop.

"Hey! I was watching that."

"You've watched enough TV over the last few days to put a small child in a coma. Get up. We're going for a walk."

"I'm sick," I whine.

Dad folds his meaty arms across his chest, his coaching voice bumping shoulders with his regular voice. "I know sick and I know self-pity. And this is a pity party if I've ever seen one."

"So?" I roll onto my side like a blanket burrito. "I lost my boyfriend and swimming in the same week. I think I'm entitled to some self-pity."

"That's why I didn't drag you out of bed yesterday." Dad flips on the light, and I bury my face in the pillow. "Meet me downstairs in five minutes."

"Dad!"

"Five minutes or you're doing push-ups," he calls on his way down the stairs.

He could be bluffing, but I decide not to risk it. When I meet Dad downstairs exactly six minutes later, my shoes are on but untied and my hair looks like Mom's snake plant, spiked in the front and flat in the back.

Huck sees my sneakers and immediately perks up. He paces the kitchen, panting, as Dad pushes a cup of coffee across the counter. "When was the last time you showered?"

I glare at him.

"Okay." His nose wrinkles slightly. "Drink up."

Mom carries her mug into the kitchen for a refill.

"Mom," I beg. "Tell him to leave me alone."

"I think some fresh air might actually make you feel better," she says, adding creamer to a fresh pour.

"So this was your idea?"

She gives a noncommittal shrug. Dad slings his arm across her shoulders. "We're your parents, Tess," he says in a made-for-TV-movie voice. "We operate as a team."

"I hate you both."

"Want some breakfast?" Mom asks cheerfully, as I lace up my sneakers and pull my hair into a knot.

"No," I snap. "If you want me to go on this stupid walk, Dad, it's now or never."

After a week spent inside, even the gray sky is blinding. I blink like a mole, shielding my eyes. Last night's rain broke the heat wave, and the air feels damp and unseasonably cool. Our neighborhood is quiet, everyone in their right mind still lounging in their pj's. Huck snuffles the sidewalk, leading the way.

To Dad's credit, he doesn't try to make me talk. Instead, he critiques the neighborhood—Mr. Mitchell's new siding is long overdue; a few people need to mow. We follow a circuitous loop, and Dad doesn't question me when we double back to avoid Charlie's house.

"I wonder how many steps that was," Dad muses as we near home. I bite back a smile; Mom may have been trying to kill two birds with one stone by suggesting a walk.

He checks his watch. "Want to go get some pancakes? I think we earned them, don't you?"

I start to say I'd prefer a sleeve of crackers and my bed thank you very much, then realize it's not actually true. My headache has dulled a little, my body feels loose and relaxed, and my stomach growls. "I could go for pancakes."

Dad grins. "I'll go get my keys."

We get to Billy's ahead of the breakfast rush and choose a quiet booth in the back.

"So..." Dad says, toying with the fluttery edge of his napkin as we wait for our pancakes. His awkward hesitation is a dead giveaway and I cut him off before the conversation gets serious.

"I agreed to pancakes, Dad, not a lecture."

His eyes widen. "Who says I was going to lecture?"

"You're seriously trying to tell me Mom didn't send you out with a mission this morning?"

"She did," Dad admits. "It was 'get Tess some fresh air.' Mission accomplished."

I thumb the thick handle of my mug. "Fine, then. What?"

"I just want to know why you're giving up on swimming."

"Dad!" When I broke the news that I'd quit the team, he promised me we didn't have to talk until I was ready. Which I'm not.

"It's not a lecture, Tess. It's a question. Swimming's been your whole life—our entire family's life—since you were in middle school. Your mom and I have sacrificed a lot..."

"I know, okay?"

Dad holds up his hand. "Hang on. That doesn't mean you can't change your mind. I want you to be happy, so let's be clear about that. But you don't seem real happy right now, and I don't think it's too much to ask to talk about it a little."

I press my spine against the booth's sticky pleather and fold my arms across my chest. "I don't really know what there is to talk about. People with epilepsy don't swim."

Dad's brows push together. "You've been swimming all summer."

"Yeah, with Davis clucking over me like a mother hen."

"So?"

"How's that going to look at Nationals? Am I going to swim in the outside lane there, too? Plus, with less speedwork, I don't even know if I'm ready."

"So it's all or nothing?" Dad asks. "Do you really feel like making B or C Finals would be worse than not competing at all?"

"I'm going to lose my scholarship either way."

"Short stack?" The waitress returns to our table, carrying a plate in each hand. It's the same woman that waited on me and Charlie at the beginning of the summer. I wonder if she remembers me. I wonder if she's looking for Charlie.

"Right here," I tell her, moving my mug out of the way.

"Then I guess the tall stack is for you," she says to Dad.

"Every last bite." The pancakes provide a brief reprieve from Dad's interrogation. After nothing but soup and saltines, my stomach opens up like a gaping black hole.

With a half stack of pancakes left on his plate, Dad wipes his hands on his napkin and leans back.

"Full?" I ask.

"Your mother says I should only eat half of what's on my plate at a restaurant. It's a good way to cut calories."

"I don't think it works that way when the other half of your plate was six pancakes."

He shoots me a look over the lip of his mug, and I laugh.

"Okay, I just need to say one more thing, and then I'll let this go," Dad says.

"About pancakes?" I tease.

"About swimming."

"Fine."

"Here's how I see it: the only way you know you'll fail is if you don't compete at all. Second to that, anything's possible."

"That's the problem," I say. "Ever since I was little, I knew how my life would play out. I could see it, crystal clear. Moving forward without a plan feels too risky." I drop my fork, suddenly wishing I was still in bed, a safe distance from Dad and this little heart-to-heart I never asked to have.

Dad scratches his chin. "I think I might be at fault here. Professional athletics has always been my dream—"

"*Our* dream," I correct him.

"Yes," Dad says. "I've steered you toward it your whole life."

"Because I wanted you to. If you don't have your eyes on the win, someone else does."

"Except sometimes life throws you a curveball, and winning becomes less important than being able to catch it." Dad picks up his mug and drains it with one swallow. "I never dreamed of being a postman, you know? If I'd known my knee was going to go, I would've done anything to avoid all that pain. Not knowing meant I played my heart out, and I loved every second of my time on the field."

"Do you miss it?" I ask.

"Sometimes," Dad says. "But you, your sister, and your mom—you were always my plan A. I just didn't know it at first."

My throat feels narrow, like a piece of pancake is stuck halfway down. I sip lukewarm coffee, but the lump doesn't go away.

"Look, Tess, if you don't love swimming anymore, I'll support you. But if you give up on your dreams before you even have a chance to chase them, you'll never know what life has in store."

"I really should've ordered wine to go with all this cheesiness."

"Are you kidding? That was the best pep talk I've ever given!"

"It was all right," I admit. "But don't tell Mom I said that."

Dad laughs. "Speaking of your mother, she's probably anxious for us to get back. You ready?"

"Yeah."

He stands and pulls his wallet from his back pocket. "You don't actually drink wine, right?"

"Seriously, Dad?"

"Just checking."

———

At home, I find the Post-it from Dr. Cappalano stuck to a book on my desk. The paper is crumpled from the trip home in my pocket, but I can still read her writing. I never really thought of myself as someone who would ever need (or want) to attend a support group. But try as they might, my friends and family can't relate to the vortex of fear and grief that threatens to consume me. No matter how much they love me, they just don't understand.

Maybe these people will.

CHAPTER
TWENTY-ONE

My last trip to the hospital was by ambulance. Tonight, my sister drives me, but the hot-rubber smell of diesel still wafts through my memory as we pass the emergency entrance. I want to curl into my fear, but Ali's voice—low, like she's waking me up—tugs me out. "Do you know where you're going?" she asks, parking the car outside the medical office entrance.

"I'll figure it out."

"I could come in with you."

"It's okay." I climb out of the car, then hesitate. "Don't go anywhere, though, okay? Just in case it's weird?"

Ali winces. "Does Starbucks count as 'anywhere'? It might be a long hour."

"Fine. Coffee and then come right back."

She gives me a thumbs-up. "Just text me when you're ready."

It's cold inside, and the plastic-bleach smell permeates even this side of the hospital, where the floor is carpeted and there are more offices than treatment bays. A security guard helps me find the conference room number scrawled on the Post-it. The walls are glass; people are seated in a circle, just like on TV. I almost bail, text Ali to abort coffee mission and come back stat, but then the security guard opens the door and everyone turns around to look at me and there's nothing I can do but take a step inside.

"Um, hi," I say, with a half-hearted wave. My eyes flit around the circle, settling on a surprisingly familiar face—the athletic director from the YMCA. "Sports Guy?"

Laughter skips around the group, and my cheeks immediately ignite. "I mean, Ian."

Recognition lights up his face. "Hi, Tess. Welcome!" He gestures to an empty seat between a girl with purple hair and a reed-tall guy with thick-rimmed glasses.

"I'm Chris," the guy says, offering his hand. "You have epilepsy?"

"Duh," pipes up the purple-haired girl. "People don't come for the cookies, Chris." Her dark eyes are thickly lined, cat-eyed at the corners. "Though I do come for the scenery," she whispers, glancing pointedly at Ian.

I smirk.

"I'm Lisette," she says. "It sucks you're here."

"Yeah," I say, startled by her blatant honesty. "It does."

"Since Tess is new, would everybody be cool with going around and introducing themselves?" Ian asks.

We take turns, each person telling me their name and why they're in the group. Most of them are around my age, with a few in their twenties, like Ian. Some, like Chris, were diagnosed as children, their seizures long managed by medication. A few are recent additions, like me. A handful of people have visible signs of a long medical journey: one guy has a jagged scar above his ear; another girl is in a wheelchair. But for the most part, people's physical appearances say more about their personalities than their diagnoses.

I'm the last to introduce myself. "I'm Tess," I say, my palms prickling with sweat. "But I guess you already knew that."

Lisette snorts.

"I had my first seizure this summer, and then another a couple weeks ago. I guess you could say it's pretty much turned my life upside down."

"Did they start you on meds?" Chris asks.

"Yeah. They kind of make me feel like crap."

A couple people nod.

"That should pass," a woman offers from across the room.

"And if it doesn't, there are other meds," someone else adds.

My stomach flip-flops; I want my turn to be over, but I have so much more to say. "I'm a swimmer," I blurt. "Or I used to be. I guess my first seizure could've killed me, but instead I lost the sport I love." A tremor creeps into my voice, and the room blurs. "Sometimes, I'm not sure which one is worse."

It's quiet for a moment. I stare at my hands, thumb away my tears.

"Dying," Lisette says.

I look up at her.

"Dying would definitely be worse."

As others share, I find I'm not alone in my grief or frustration. One person suffered a seizure at work and now feels like her boss treats her differently. Another recently lost his license and just switched to a third medication because the first two haven't worked. But joy, hope, and even empowerment are also present: A woman flashes her engagement ring to a round of cheering and whistles. A handful of people have worked as counselors at a nearby summer camp for children with epilepsy. They swap funny and heartwarming stories. Chris tells us about the presentation on epilepsy safety awareness he's been giving at local schools.

"I had these made, too." He tugs at his purple T-shirt. 1 IN 26, it says, in bold, block lettering.

"What's it mean?" I ask.

"One in every twenty-six people could develop epilepsy at some point in their life," Chris explains. "Not enough people understand it, even though statistics say it will affect someone they know."

"Maybe you should give one of your presentations at my work," the first woman says.

"Anytime."

"Can I get one of those?" Lisette asks, eyeing the purple T-shirt, only a few shades darker than her hair. "The color's calling to me."

Chris grins. "I brought a box."

After group, people linger, chatting over cookies and lemonade. "So how do you know Ian?" Lisette asks.

"He works with my boy—" The word cuts off in my throat, followed by a stab of regret. "I met him at the Y."

"Small world, huh?" Ian says as the conversation shifts away from us.

"Charlie didn't say anything."

"He wouldn't know. I haven't had a seizure for years, but I do wear this." Ian tugs a thin gold chain from his shirt, a dog tag dangling at the end. "Medical ID. Just in case."

I nibble at my cookie, unsure what to say next.

Ian clears his throat. "If you ever want to use the pool at the Y, it's typically pretty empty around one."

"Oh, I don't—"

"Just wanted to make sure you know," he says.

I leave with one of Chris's T-shirts, Lisette's number, and a group invitation to go bowling in a few weeks.

"Guess it went okay?" Ali asks when I climb into the car.

"Yeah," I say, toying with the purple T-shirt in my lap. *One in twenty-six.* "It really did."

It's the middle of the afternoon, and I'm lying on the couch, half watching a show about teen pregnancy, which is only making me feel a little better about my crap life. Everyone I know is either busy or at work, and while my ex-teammates will be heading to practice in a few hours, I'll go through the motions of yet another evening at home with my family: dinner, dishes, cop show reruns, bed. More like the routine of a seventy-year-old than a seventeen-year-old. The side effects of my medication have slowly begun to subside, which means my daily walks with Huck aren't cutting it anymore. The lack of exercise leaves me fidgety and agitated, longing for a real workout in the water.

I glance at the clock. If I hurry, I can make it to the YMCA while the pool's still empty. A quick text to Mac confirms Charlie's at the swim club, so I won't have to worry about running into him. Though the fee is a hit to my bank account, I schedule the Uber ride and head upstairs to change.

When I arrive in Ian's office, he greets me with a smile. "Tess! Did you come for a swim or a job? I've got both available."

"Just a swim," I tell him. "If that's still okay?"

"Let's go check it out."

Ian has me fill out a guest form and then takes me to the pool. One lane is occupied by a lap swimmer; the lifeguard swings her whistle in a bored circle. "Looks like it's all yours," Ian says, glancing at the clock. "For at least the next thirty minutes."

I head to the locker room, returning with my hot-pink cap and towel. The lifeguard suddenly seems more attentive, and I know Ian spoke to her, that she's on high alert for signs of a seizure.

Noodles, life jackets, and other swim lesson gear wait by the side of the wall, along with the rubber duckies I used to coax that little girl into the water. As a kid, I didn't need coaxing. Dad called me his fish; Mom, her little mermaid. And after one underwater tea party that lasted uncomfortably long, Ali checked behind my ears for gills. Now, as I step into the water, the ripples carry back the flash of red lights and the sound of my teammates' tears. Proof that I'm not a mermaid and I don't have gills. That breathing underwater is impossible.

The lifeguard smiles encouragingly, disrupting the memory of that night and pushing back my mounting anxiety. As I stretch out into an easy freestyle, my body seems to sigh in relief, like slipping into freshly cleaned sheets or melting into a hug.

Reach, pull.

Breathe.

My mind twists around one in twenty-six like an equation that doesn't quite add up. With numbers like that, there must be people with epilepsy at school, even at Northern Hills. A huge community of people whose differences are largely invisible, like superheroes whose power is survival, showing up, living fully no matter what.

I have wasted so much time striving toward a vision of the perfect future, like there's a right path and a wrong one. Epilepsy has thrown out the map altogether. But it hasn't taken away my choices, and it doesn't mean my life is over. As I ease into a familiar workout that leaves my heart racing with joy, I remember that the human body is 70 percent water, that we're basically breathing underwater all the time.

CHAPTER
TWENTY-TWO

My room is dark when my alarm clock wakes me up Saturday. The welcome smell of coffee wafts up the stairs, and my body twitches eagerly at the thought of swimming. I send a quick text to Mac:

Tess: **Can I get a ride to practice?**
Mac: **Yasss girl!**

And then the unicorn farting emoji, because she's Mac and because why not.

Dad's in the kitchen when I jog down for breakfast. He glances at my workout clothes, surprise lighting up his face.

"Going for a jog?"

"Mac's picking me up for practice," I say, filling a travel mug.

"Did I miss something?"

"A ton," I tease. "Next time, try to keep up, okay?"

Dad runs his hand across his head, spiking up his hair like a bewildered baby porcupine. "Okay."

A car horn blasts through the quiet of the morning, announcing Mac's arrival. I slap together a peanut butter sandwich and toss a coconut water into my gym bag, right next to the medicine I'll need to take in a few hours. Dad follows me to the front door. "Proud of you, girl."

"Thanks, Dad."

———

Mac and I walk together down the darkened hallway toward Coach's office. "If she turns me down, I'll call my mom to pick me up," I say.

"She's not going to turn you down." Mac opens the locker room door; fluorescent light and sleepy morning voices spill into the hall. "Come tell me after," she says. "No matter what."

I take a deep breath and tap my knuckles against Coach's open door. She glances up from her computer. "Cooper?"

"I was wondering if it's okay for me to practice with the team today?"

"Just for today?"

"I'm not actually sure." My voice is too small, too high-pitched.

Coach steeples her fingers. "I can't have you hopping on and off the team whenever you feel like it, Cooper. You're either in or you're out."

"Do I have to decide now?"

"Before you show up to practice, yes," she says. "I'm happy to work with you however I need to. But if you quit again, there's no coming back."

No matter how hard I peer into the future, the images ahead are blurry blotches of uncertainty. I might lose my scholarship. I might get hurt.

I might not.

All I have to go on is the smell of chlorine and the stirring in my heart.

"I'm in," I say before I can regret it.

172

"Good." Coach's eyes shift back to her computer. "Go get changed."

In the locker room, a few stragglers hurry out of their clothes and fumble with their swim caps. Mac waits by my locker, dressed and ready for practice. "Well?"

I muster a weak smile. "I'm back."

"Then why do you sound like she told you to go dig your own grave?"

My shoulders collapse like a caving dam; the truth rushes out. "She said I had to decide—if I quit again, I'm off for good. I just sort of reacted, but I don't know if I can face the rest of the team, and..."

"Tess." Mac puts her hands on my shoulders, quelling the rising panic. "Breathe."

Inhale. Exhale.

"True or false. Ready?"

I close my eyes. "Ready."

"You love to swim."

"True."

"You want to swim at Northern Hills."

"True," I whisper.

"You want to go to Nationals."

"But what if—"

"No what-ifs. Just true or false."

I imagine what it would be like to stay behind while Rachel and Mac and all the others go to Nationals. The feeling that floods my chest isn't relief. It's regret. "True," I say. "I want to go."

Mac's smile fills her words. "Then it doesn't matter what anybody else thinks. This is about you and the water. You can't win if you don't swim."

The locker room door slams open and Rachel's voice slices

through the air. "Mac, Coach is about to have a conniption—" Her eyes settle on me. "Oh."

"Hey, Rach," I say.

She tips her chin. "You're back?"

"I am."

"And Nationals?"

"That's the plan."

Rachel's lips twist, her eyes drilling into me. "Good," she says finally. "Hurry up." The door slams heavily behind her.

When Mac and I join the team beside the pool, warm-up has already begun. A few swimmers cast curious glances my way. But there's nothing for me to prove anymore and nothing else to hide.

Mac squeezes my elbow, hurrying past as Davis approaches. "We're running relays today. I threw together a workout for you." He waves a piece of scratch paper.

It'd be stupid to practice at race pace on my first day back. While the rest of my team gets to wrap their brains and bodies around the thrill of the championship events ahead, I'll spend the next two hours in a steady aerobic pace.

Inhale. Exhale.

Reach. Pull.

"Give me the rundown," I say.

He fills me in on the drills he's planned. "It's good to have you back, Cooper."

"It's good to be back."

Swimming is the easy part. Being myself is harder, and I've never been one to turn down a challenge.

CHAPTER
TWENTY-THREE

"So those tiny little pills are really making all the difference, huh?" Mac asks.

"So far so good." I toss back my meds as Mom places a platter of glistening corn on the cob on the table. Dad's grilling, and Mac's staying for dinner after practice. "That and avoiding 'triggers,'" I say, framing the word in finger quotations. Plenty of healthy food? Check. Staying hydrated? Check. Nine hours of sleep? Check. I'm learning that so much about epilepsy is waiting and hoping and doing your best. On the plus side, between all this self-care and training, I've barely had time to think about Charlie.

Barely.

"Here's to magic little pills," Mac says, toasting the air with her glass of lemonade.

"Cheers to that," Ali says, joining us at the table.

We eat grilled chicken, corn, and salad, and then linger outside, enjoying the cool evening air until the first fireflies prick the dusk like flickering stars. "You girls feeling ready?" Dad asks. He doesn't say what for, but with Nationals less than two weeks away, it's all he can talk about.

"Already packed," Mac says. "The win doesn't wait, sir."

Dad chuckles at his own axiom. "Attagirl."

I smirk, knowing Mac will still be throwing things into her suitcase on the morning of our flight.

"What about you?" Ali asks, tapping my leg under the table.

"I still have to get my suit." Even though I had to quit my job at the Sugar Shack to make time for extra practices with Coach and rest in between, my savings will cover the same brand of suit I get every year. It'll be last year's model, but at least I'll know it works.

"I can take you later this week," Ali says. "But that's not really what I meant."

"Nervous," I admit, remembering the cheer that had gone up in support group this week when I'd shared about going to Nationals. Funny how fear of a thing can sometimes make you want it all that much more.

"Don't get me started," Mom says, rising to collect our plates. They clatter dangerously.

Mac's eyes follow Mom into the house. "Is she okay?"

"Depends on what you mean by *okay*," Ali deadpans.

To Mom's credit, she'd tried to appear happy when I'd told my family about my decision to rejoin the team. But over the last week, the tension in our house has prickled like static electricity threatening a storm. Dad pushes back his chair. "I'll talk to her."

"I got it, Dad," I say.

Mom's at the kitchen sink, running hot water over the dishes. "Mom—"

"I don't want to talk about it." She squirts soap too hard; a small blue puddle pools over her sponge. "You've made your decision; I said I support you, and I do. But it doesn't mean I have to be happy about it."

"Can I at least help?" I ask.

"Suit yourself."

I open the dishwasher, load plates and glasses one at a time. Mom attacks the greasy corn platter. "I just don't understand why at least one of my girls doesn't want a nice, regular job," she says. "Like a real estate agent or a dental hygienist."

My lip curls at the thought of scraping dirty teeth. "Gross."

"You know what I mean." Mom's exhale puffs the hair that's fallen around her face. "You and your sister were both born with so much potential—beautiful, smart, creative. There is so much life in front of you and so many ways that life can hurt you. All I've ever wanted is for you both to be safe and happy."

"Those things don't always go together," I say, the truth of the words settling deep in my chest.

Mom peers at me, her forehead shiny with steam.

"Our version of happy might not look the way you think it should. If you really want us to be happy, you have to let go of trying to keep us safe."

The ferocity written in the sharp lines of Mom's face briefly softens. On the smooth surface, I read confusion and loss. And then it's gone, like a book slammed shut, and Mom turns back to the dishes.

———

"Two-oh-two," Coach says, tapping her watch. "Not bad. Not bad at all."

I lean against the side of the pool, chest heaving. My teammates crash through the water in the other lanes, their hearts and bodies stretched almost to the limit. It's my first goal time swim since my seizure, and the whole time I expected to suddenly find myself on the deck, staring into Davis's closed eyes as he gives me mouth-to-mouth. The thought makes me shudder—for more than one reason—and I push out into an easy backstroke, letting my heart rate lower and the fear subside.

Coach walks the length of the pool, her clipboard tapping against the side of her leg. "How do you feel?" she asks, and I can't help but wonder if she, too, was waiting for me to buckle and convulse, waiting for the moment when she would have to dive in and save me.

"Good, I guess."

"You looked good. I know you're worried about time, but if you keep this up, I think you're going to surprise yourself."

Time isn't the only thing I'm worried about. It used to be just me and the water when I raced. Now it's me, the water, and epilepsy. And there isn't room for the three of us in my head—especially not at Nationals.

Coach waits with my towel when I'm finished cooling down. "As far as I can tell, the only thing your seizures took from you was confidence. Unfortunately, that's going to be the hardest thing to get back."

I pull off my goggles and press my face into my towel.

"I finally heard back from the board rep," Coach says, referencing the call she'd made last week about my participation at Nationals. "They've agreed to make some accommodations for us." She ticks them off like items on a packing list. "You'll be swimming in the outer lane for all races. That's going to be a time disadvantage, so we'll need to prepare for that. They've hired an extra lifeguard to keep eyes on you at all times. And they've given us one of the pace lanes—"

"A pace lane?"

"We need it if you're going to be able to practice safely."

"Yeah, but..." The pace lanes are the outer lanes of warm-up pools, used for practice in the days leading up to finals. Typically reserved for goal time swims, pace lanes are precious real estate for a swimmer and her coach to work one-on-one. Now there will be one less available, and it won't take long for everyone to figure out why. "Is that really necessary?"

"What's the problem, Cooper?"

Water drips like sweat down my forehead. "If you thought that guy at Mountain Ridge was bad…"

"Think about it this way," Coach says. "The man I spoke to seemed almost excited about the accommodations they're making. I think this has created an opportunity for them to think about inclusivity. You're not the first swimmer with epilepsy, and you won't be the last. You're helping to pave the way."

"What if I don't want the attention?" As much as I admire Chris from group, who's making schools safer for people with epilepsy just by showing up and using his voice, I don't have his brand of courage. The only attention I want at Nationals is the kind that comes when you win.

Coach zeroes in on my fear. "You're not going to be able to fly under the radar. You know that, right? People are going to know what happened. Wes Andrews is going to know what happened. That's going to have to be okay with you."

A lump forms in my throat at the mention of my future college coach. "What if it's not?"

"It might not be up to you."

Mac scoops me up on her way to the locker room. "What were you and Coach talking about?" she asks. "It looked serious."

"Turns out you're looking at this year's poster child for competitive swimmers with epilepsy." I yank my flip-flops out of my gym bag.

"So in this metaphor, you're the swimmer and the mascot?" Rachel fluffs her hair in front of the mirror. "Do you get to wear a giant head?"

I shoot her a scalding glare.

"I'm guessing you don't want the attention," Mac says.

"I just don't want to have epilepsy," I mutter, slamming my locker door.

Mac gives me a small, sad smile. "But you do."

———

Mac drops me off after practice, and I'm digging my key out of my gym bag when a familiar voice takes me by surprise. "Tess, hey!"

I drop the key, awkwardly twisting around to face Charlie. Of all the scenarios I've imagined over the last couple of weeks, my first post-breakup encounter with Charlie definitely wasn't supposed to look like this: him shirtless and drenched in sweat, like some kind of muscly sun god, and me with chlorine-stiff hair, literally squatting on my front stoop. "Um...hey."

Charlie pulls out his earbuds and jogs across my lawn. The forward momentum in his shoulders warns of a hug, but he stops just short of reaching out.

I want him to hug me. I want to press my face against his chest, sweat and all.

"You haven't been at work."

"I had to quit. I'm swimming again—we head to Nationals next week."

Charlie's mouth curves into a sideways smile. "Why am I not surprised?"

"Yeah," I say, my cheeks suddenly hot.

Charlie lifts his earbuds, but I'm not ready for him to walk away. Too much of our story is still unwritten and I don't know how to turn back the pages. So I start at the beginning. "Do you want to come in?" I ask. "I make a mean scrambled egg."

Charlie squints at me. "No green stuff, right?"

"Wouldn't dream of it."

"Then I'm in."

We take our breakfast to the deck: a veggie omelet for me and scrambled eggs with a few pieces of Dad's secret bacon for Charlie. Huck snoozes under the table between our feet. We talk about small things—how Taro jacked up all the prices in the Sugar Shack and how Howie has a new girlfriend at the YMCA. We don't talk about big things. We don't talk about seizures, or parents, or us.

Charlie balls his napkin onto his plate and leans back in his chair. "That was pretty good. You can add 'chef' to your extensive list of talents."

"Don't get too excited. Pretty sure a person can't live off of eggs and peanut butter."

"Says who?"

"Right—I forgot I'm talking to a guy who considers pancakes a food group."

Charlie laughs, and the sound is so familiar it makes my heart ache. I want to make him laugh again. I never want to make him feel any other way.

"Howie got some good news," he says. "He was accepted into college."

I gape at him.

"He'll take regular classes and everything. There's a special support program for people with Down syndrome. He'll learn how to live by himself, get a job, stuff like that."

"Wow—that's so cool." I picture Charlie's family in the stands at Howie's graduation, watching as he crosses the stage. Then I think about Howie and Charlie in the stands at my meet, and I blink away unexpected tears.

Suddenly, I want nothing more than to go back to that night at the carnival, to stay in the car, to ride out the storm. Words rush out, unchecked. "I'm sorry for the things I said, Charlie. I never should've pushed you about your dad. It wasn't my business, and I—"

"I pushed you, too." Charlie's thick brows inch together. "You lost the thing most important to you, and I didn't know how to help. I'm not…I guess I'm not good with stuff like that."

I stare at Charlie's hands, large enough to engulf my own, and I think about the twinkle lights in his living room window, the glow of fireworks on his skin. How he never made me feel normal, how he always made me feel extraordinary. In the haze of early morning, I believe that it's possible: that my life is big enough for pain and joy, that love is the most important thing.

"I just wish…" I fumble.

"Tess." Charlie leans forward.

"If I could go back, I'd—"

"Tess, I'm moving."

A fissure spreads between my feet, and the world collapses into it.

Charlie's face is pained, his tone apologetic. "I've been sitting here trying to figure out how to tell you. My mom got a job a few hours away. She wants to get Max settled before school starts, so she's headed out next week to find a place."

"And you?" I choke.

The look Charlie gives me feels full of longing. Or maybe that's just what I want to see. "I guess I'm still trying to figure things out."

I think about Charlie's dad—the phone calls Charlie ignores and the past he can't let go of. He does have a lot to figure out, and as much as I want to, I can't do it for him.

"I should go," Charlie says, reaching for my plate. "I have work soon." We carry our dishes into the kitchen, and then I walk Charlie to the door.

"We'll stay in touch, right?"

"We can try," says Charlie. "Maybe I'll even show up at one of your races with another poster, just to keep you on your toes."

I wince. The next time I'll race is at Nationals, where placing in the A Finals will bring me closer to the life I've always dreamed of—but even further away from Charlie.

"For the record," he says, just before we part, "I wish we could go back, too." He lopes across my yard, and I stay on the stoop, trying to catch my breath.

CHAPTER
TWENTY-FOUR

Three days before Nationals, I'm checking (and rechecking) the growing contents of my suitcase, making sure I'm prepared for the week away from home. The T-shirt Chris gave me is folded on my desk, still unworn. I add it to the pile—a reminder that even across the country, away from my family and the support of my group, I'm not alone.

I'm getting ready for bed when Mom knocks softly on my door. "Can I come in?"

"Sure."

She holds a plastic bag behind her back.

"What's that?" I ask.

The bag is from SwimSwam, the store where we've always gotten my gear. I take it, my heart rate tipping up at the glimpse of black and red spandex inside.

"What did you—"

Mom sinks onto the end of my bed as I pull out the suit, the newest model of my favorite brand, costing well over $500. I wouldn't have been able to afford it until next year, when a newer one will be released. The soft light in my room glances off the suit's red racing stripe, and I can't wait to put it on. "Mom!" I exclaim.

"You've been working so hard," she says. "And after everything..." Her breath hitches. "You've always worked hard. This summer, I've realized how courageous you are. Certainly braver than me."

Suddenly, she seems so small, so vulnerable. I lunge, fling my arms around her, and press my cheek against the top of her head, breathing her in.

"I do want you to be happy," she says. "Even if it scares me."

My eyes fill, and I drop down beside her, leaning my head onto her shoulder. "Thank you."

Her cool hand rests against my cheek. "Just promise me you'll be careful."

Even in the safety of my bedroom with Mom beside me, the only feelings within reach are fear and uncertainty. "I will," I whisper, for her benefit and my own.

———

The tension in the van on the way to the airport is suffocating. "It's going to be great," Dad says randomly, adjusting his hands on the steering wheel. He drives like he just got his license, hands at ten and two; he checks his rearview and side mirrors obsessively, even looks over his shoulder before he turns. Mom sips her coffee in silence.

It's been like this for the last three days. My parents have never come to Nationals with me—the extra plane tickets, not to mention five days in a hotel, have always been more than we could afford. Though it's never bothered me before, traveling across the country without my parents now fills me with an undercurrent of dread, and I know they feel the same way.

"Want me to park?" Dad asks, as we take the airport exit off I-95. His eyes meet mine in the rearview.

"Of course," Mom says.

"No," I tell them. It was hard enough leaving Ali in the driveway. If my parents get out, if I hug them, I might not be able to let go.

Mom twists around in her seat. "Are you sure?"

"I'm sure." I pull my suitcase closer as Dad edges up to the curb.

"Stay in the car, please!" the curb attendant shouts.

"Did you set a timer to take your meds?" Mom asks.

"Yes."

"What about snacks?"

I motion to my backpack, the same one Mom filled with enough protein bars to energize my entire team. "I've got it all, Mom." My voice is thick with exhaustion, fear, and tears. "I love you guys."

Mom makes a squeaking noise, and Dad reaches around to squeeze my knee. "Listen to me, kid. All you can do is your best. No matter how it turns out, we are so incredibly proud of you."

"I know," I manage.

"Call us," Mom chokes. "Every night, okay?"

"I will, I promise."

"You getting out or what?" the curb attendant demands.

I climb out of the van and drag my luggage behind me. The wheels hit the curb, and I wonder if it's too late to jump back in, go home with my parents, and hide in bed for the next five days. Dad edges the van back into the slow flow of traffic and honks twice to say goodbye.

I spot Coach at the gate before I see the rest of the team. She's pacing, her fingers wrapped rigidly around what is likely one-too-many cups of coffee, and she checks her watch every five minutes. She gets like this every year—she's been threatening to leave us in the airport for the last week.

My teammates huddle over paper coffee cups and flip through their phones. Amal and Seth are sound asleep, their heads propped on their backpacks. I sink into the empty seat beside Rachel. She pulls out an earbud and smirks at me. "You showed."

"Barely." I drop my backpack on the floor between my knees.

"I'm coming, I'm coming!" Mac flies toward us, her hair unbrushed, her backpack bouncing, and a Frap sloshing out of its lid.

Coach rolls her eyes. "You're late."

"Only a little," Mac squeaks, sinking into the seat beside me. Even though it's already eighty-five degrees, she's wearing sweats and fuzzy slippers. As soon as the wheels lift off the ground, she'll curl into a cozy ball and fall dead asleep.

I lean my shoulder against hers, anxiety subsiding. Whatever happens this week, I won't have to face it alone.

We land in California tired and achy. Coach herds us like sluggish cats onto the hotel shuttle. After seven hours of sitting, it's critical we hit the pool as soon as possible to flush the lactic acid from our systems in preparation for the few days of practice before finals.

In the lobby, Coach hands out our room keys. Mac and I are with Rachel, and Lily and Simone are together. "You have forty-five minutes to unpack," Coach says. "If you're not on the shuttle, I'm leaving you behind."

"If you're not on the shuttle..." Mac grumbles in a high-pitched whisper.

I push her away before Coach hears.

"Yo," Seth says in the elevator, "wanna hit the hot tub tonight? I hear it's on the roof."

I roll my eyes. Seth's gotten busted for partying at Nationals so many times I'm surprised Coach even let him come this year. I guess since the school's gym is named after his parents, her hands are pretty much tied.

Amal leans closer to Rachel. "What do you say, babe? You, me, hot tub?"

She elbows him in the stomach, and he doubles over to the sleep-deprived amusement of everybody else.

The elevator chimes, and we all tumble out. The boys head down the hall in one direction, and we girls head the opposite way. Mac slides the key in and Rachel shoves past her, belly-flopping onto the first bed. "Dibs on sleeping alone!"

Mac drags her suitcase to the far corner of the room. "You're such a bitch sometimes," she grumbles.

Rachel crosses her arms behind her head and nestles farther into the queen-sized bed. "Yeah, but not for no reason."

We unpack, change into our track suits, and head down to meet Coach in the lobby. Lily and Simone are taking selfies, and if I had to guess, Seth and Amal are already planning tonight's rooftop party. Part of me can't blame them. Their entire futures don't hinge on the outcome of this trip.

Coach waves us all into the shuttle. "How are you feeling, Cooper?" she asks.

"Nervous," I admit.

"I was hoping for confident." She gives me a wry smile, but the look in her eyes gives her away. Coach is nervous for me, too.

———

The university hosting Nationals is absolutely gorgeous. Four outdoor pools gleam turquoise under a cloudless sky. Several teams are already in the water, and we check out our competition on the way to the locker rooms. Swimming clubs and colleges from across the country have brought their best swimmers, many of whom are gunning for a shot at Olympic Trials. A flash of maroon and gold, Northern Hills' colors, draws my eye. Wes Andrews, my future coach, talks with too-big hand gestures to the swimmers circled around him. As my teammates' voices dip and rise, all I can think about is where I'll be swimming and how long it will take before everyone here—especially Coach Andrews—knows why.

When I step out of the locker room, Coach Higgins is talking to one of the event officials, a short man with a thick mustache that twitches like a mouse as Coach lays into him. "I was told a pace lane would be closed for us," she says. "I have a swimmer that needs the outer lane. I thought this had already been handled."

Suddenly, my new suit feels like it's tugging on my shoulder blades.

"What's going on?" Mac asks.

"They're closing down a pace lane," I tell her. "Because of me."

Her eyes widen.

"I know."

"This way," the official says, sufficiently worn down. He leads us to a pool at the far end of the deck, where the rest of our crew has already staked out a warm-up spot. Their gear and water bottles create a boundary we'll try to protect over the next week. Rachel lies on the ground, rolling out her quads, while the other swimmers stretch.

The warm-up lanes are already crowded, full of arms and legs that thrash through the water, trying not to kick someone else in the face. Pace lanes are such precious commodities that pools usually only allow each swimmer a lap or two before it's someone else's turn. By the time the rest of the teams gets here, the loss of even one pace lane will throw a wrench in everyone's practice plans.

The official heads down the lane to speak with the other coaches, taking with him any hope I'd had of sliding under the radar this week. Coach Higgins reviews our practice plan, and my teammates enter the pool one at a time, like cars merging onto a busy highway. I slip into the pace lane and push out into the water, pretending not to notice the other swimmers, whose stares and whispers skip across the surface like stones.

———

The hotel dining area buzzes with excitement and anticipation: tomorrow is the first day of finals. Tonight's practice invigorated everyone, reminding us what speed and winning taste like. We'd grabbed takeout salads on the way back to the hotel. Clustered on one side of the dining room, we're reviewing the event schedule and checking in with Coach about the best plan of action for managing our various events.

Rachel spreads the schedule out across the table. Over the next five days, she and I will both compete in all the freestyle events, including a distance swim and the relay. Rachel runs her finger down tomorrow's lineup. "The 100 is back-to-back with the 800," she tells me over a mouthful of chicken salad.

"I know." A 100-meter sprint just before a distance swim is asking for muscle fatigue and exhaustion—a big risk to take the day before we'll swim the 200-meter free.

"At least you don't have to do it twice," Mac offers. While our times at tomorrow morning's preliminary races will determine whether we compete in the A, B, C, or D Finals for the 100-meter free, there are no preliminaries for distance events. Swimming that distance twice in one day would put an athlete at an extreme disadvantage for the rest of the meet, so for distance swims, we're grouped according to our entry times.

Rachel stabs a cherry tomato. "It's a small mercy."

"Are you going to do both the 100 and the 800?" I ask her.

"Aren't you?"

I push damp lettuce around my plate, considering. Coach and I had talked about this at practice tonight. While the 800-meter free is the only event where I'm guaranteed to compete in the A Final, the lack of a preliminary swim means I won't know if I'm ready to race that distance until the moment it matters most.

"Scratching the 100 will keep me fresh for the 800," I say.

"Yeah," says Rachel, "but don't you want to get a feel for the water before the 800? It'd be pretty ballsy to go into a distance swim cold."

She has a point. Placing in the 100 meter will give me a much-needed confidence boost that will feed into the 800 meter, which—like all A Final events—will be broadcast on live TV. "You might be right."

"When am I not?"

The hotel doors slide open, and a team strolls through. Decked out in maroon and gold tracksuits, these girls are from Northern Hills. My eyes dart to the entrance, but Coach Andrews isn't with them. Relieved, I turn back to the event schedule as the girls head to the elevator.

"That's her, isn't it?" one of them whisper-shouts.

"Who?"

"The one with epilepsy. They gave her a whole pace lane to warm up."

My spine tingles; my future teammates gawk at me like a zoo animal.

Mac whirls around in her seat, but it's Rachel who snaps off first. "Get a good look. She'll be the one obliterating your time tomorrow."

One of the girls huffs indignantly. The other opens her mouth to say something, but then the elevator chimes and they scurry in.

"Rach," Mac says, staring at her. "That was actually pretty nice."

"Yeah," I say. "Thanks."

Rachel hunches over her salad. "Don't get used to it."

As we finish our dinner, I try to focus on mapping out the rest of my week. But all I can think about is those girls. Tomorrow I'm swimming against them, but next year, I hope to swim beside them. If they've already labeled me as "the one with epilepsy," what does that mean for my spot in their ranks?

CHAPTER
TWENTY-FIVE

In the morning, hundreds of swimmers on fire to compete jostle against each other on the pool deck as teams stake out their territories and begin warming up for prelims.

We drop our gear at the spot we've claimed, and begin to stretch. I'm rolling out my shoulders when Coach Higgins approaches, sipping coffee from a travel mug. "You ready for this?" she asks.

I take out one of my earbuds, already blasting my race playlist to energize me for the swim ahead. "Absolutely." Hopefully saying it out loud will make it true.

Coach follows my gaze to the other pool, where Andrews clocks a swimmer in the pace lane.

"He'll be focused on his own team," she says, reading my mind.

I raise my brow.

"Mostly," she concedes. "It doesn't matter anyway. You're ready." I grasp onto the steadiness in her voice and hold on for dear life. "Your body knows what to do. Don't let your head get you off track."

By the time my event nears, the music and movement have steadied my nerves. I head to the locker room with Rachel and

Mac to change into our race suits. A handful of Northern Hills girls eye us like prey as we look for an empty spot to change.

"Maybe they're not all like that," Mac whispers, running a towel down her damp legs.

Rachel snorts. "Yeah, they seem really nice."

Refusing to be intimidated by the intense looks aimed our way, I ease my race suit up my skin, and zip my parka over it. *You're ready,* I tell myself, and then crank up my music before my brain can say otherwise.

Mac easily secures her spot in the C Final for the 100-meter free. When it's time for our heat, Rachel and I head to the blocks and drop our towels and parkas in the waiting bins. "Make me work for it," Rachel says, lining up behind a Northern Hills swimmer, who smirks at me as I take my place at the outer lane. Swimming in this lane is a disadvantage, which the other girls are happy to give me. It means I'll have to swim faster, harder, to secure my spot in the A Final tonight.

The swimmer ahead of me climbs out of the pool, her eyes searching the clock for her time. Adrenaline surges through my veins, and I bounce on my toes, shaking out my hands. "I'm ready," I whisper under my breath. "I'm ready."

My skin prickles as I take the block. My mind traces over the race, the turn, the touchpad against my hand.

Reach.

Pull.

Breathe.

The starter buzzes and my muscles explode; I crash through the water like a shark after prey. One turn, and then my hand slaps the touchpad, and I break the surface, chest heaving. I jerk off my goggles, certain I made it into the A Final.

55:02.

Just above the cutoff.

My confidence drains like blood into the water. I hoist myself out of the pool and yank my towel from the bin, glancing around for Higgins, but it's Coach Andrews whose eyes meet mine over his own swimmer's shoulder. He pats her back and points her toward the hospitality tent where food and Gatorade wait. Then he approaches me.

"Cooper," he says.

"Coach."

"That's not what I was expecting to see from you this morning."

I swallow. "Me neither."

He works his jaw. "I hear you've had some health challenges."

"Yes, sir."

"Nothing holds my swimmers back," he says. "Nothing."

I press my towel against my mouth, breathing in bleach and failure.

"I'm expecting a lot from you. Don't let me down."

Rachel comes up behind me as Andrews turns back to his team. "That guy's got a lamppost up his ass," she says. "I mean, you didn't completely suck."

Easy for her to say—she made the A Final cutoff with time to spare. "Thanks a lot."

She shrugs. "Let's go get food."

I don't want food. I want to get the hell out of here. But I follow Rachel to the hospitality tent, barely taking in Mac's and Coach's reassurance as I choke down a bland energy bar before heading to the cooldown pool. It doesn't matter what they say. In less than sixty seconds, my worst fear has come true. No matter how hard I've worked over the last few weeks, it wasn't good enough.

—

Rachel's parents are waiting in the hotel lobby when we get back from prelims.

"I thought you weren't getting here until later," Rachel says, giving them both a quick hug. Mrs. Kolowski wears white ankle pants and a flowing floral blouse; her husband sports too-tight khaki shorts. While I'd long ago accepted that my parents couldn't possibly afford to come, seeing Rachel's parents now makes me miss mine more than ever.

Mrs. Kolowski's heavily lined eyes settle on me. "Tess, how are you feeling?"

"Fine." My voice trembles slightly.

"She just bit it at prelims," Rachel says.

"Rach!" Mac exclaims, shoving her shoulder.

"What? She did!" She looks at me expectantly, like I'm going to back her up. "You did."

Tears prick my eyes, and I blink them away.

Mrs. Kolowski clears her throat. "We came to take you to lunch," she tells Rachel. "Why don't you bring your friends?"

Rachel's eyes flit to Mac, then me, and back again. "Sure," she says with a shrug. "Why not?"

We head upstairs, but the thought of spending the next hour pretending not to feel like crap is more than I can bear, even if there is free food involved. I sit on the floor outside the bathroom, where Rachel and Mac are dabbing on lip gloss and mascara. "I'm not really up for lunch," I tell them. "I think I'd rather just be alone."

Mac turns away from the mirror, her mascara wand poised midair. "You're not coming?"

"Whatever you do," Rachel says, "you better get your mind straight. This whole misery thing"—she waves her hand at me—"is not going to work out well tonight."

Mac gives me a quick hug before joining Rachel in the hall. "You sure you don't want to come?"

"I'm sure." If I'm going to compete tonight, I need to clear my head. So I lace up my sneakers, grab my phone and earbuds, and head downstairs for a walk.

Between the cloudless sky and the humidity-free warmth, my mood improves with every block. After a while, I'm ready to call my parents.

The phone barely rings before Dad answers. His labored breath tells me he's walking one of the many neighborhoods on his route. "How'd it go?" he asks.

"Not good."

On either side of the country, Dad and I walk together as I fill him in.

"I know you're disappointed," he says, when I've finished. "But B Final is nothing to shake a stick at."

"Tell that to Coach Andrews. He said *nothing* holds his team back, Dad. I mean, he didn't say *epilepsy* specifically, but that's what he meant. If I can't get it together, I'm going to lose my scholarship, I know it."

A dog barks in the background, and Dad's voice muffles slightly as he digs in his pocket for the treats he always carries. "You can't get that far ahead of yourself, Tess. One race at time, okay?"

I take a deep breath, inhaling Dad's words like oxygen.

"I can't wait to see you swim tonight," he says. "I'm making cheese dip." The thought of my family hunched over Mom's laptop, eating chips and dip and yelling at the screen, makes me smile and also makes my chest ache.

"I love you guys."

"We loved you first," Dad says.

One race at a time, I repeat like a mantra as I turn and head back to the hotel.

CHAPTER
TWENTY-SIX

Adrenaline crackles like electricity above the water and hums in the air as I follow my team to our warm-up spot. Coaches pace the pools, issuing last-minute advice and reminders. Coach Andrews gives one of his swimmers an earful about something. Red blotches form on her face as she tries not to cry.

"Tess Cooper?" A woman steps in my path wearing street clothes and makeup; she wields a microphone like a sword. "You're Tess Cooper, right?"

I pull out my earbuds. "Um, yeah?"

Rachel snorts.

The reporter motions for her sidekick, a heavyset guy with a camera on his shoulder. She tells me they belong to a regional network covering the event. "Can we talk to you for a second?"

"Sure." The camera feels too close, and my hands instinctively dart to my hair, pushing back flyaways.

"You were ranked for the A Final, but tonight you're competing in the B Final for the 100-meter free," the woman says. "Does that have anything to do with the health challenges you've faced this summer?"

The arena closes in around me; everyone who passes seems to gawk and leer.

"Um…"

"You're also swimming in the 800-meter free tonight. Are you at all worried you may not be able to perform?"

"N-no," I stammer. "I—"

"What about the possibility of having a seizure during the race?"

The camera is too close, the air too thin.

"Excuse me—" Coach pushes past the reporter, slips her arm around my shoulders. "My swimmer needs to warm up."

The woman's lips press together; the mic falls limply to her side.

"You okay?" Coach asks, steering me away from the reporting team.

"I'm fine." But now I can't shake the feeling that the sky-high bleachers are packed with people here to see me fail.

"It's your race," Coach says. "Don't let them get in your head."

I nod tightly, as we head to the warm-up pool, where my team is trying to snag a spot.

As the C Final begins, I keep my eyes on the scoreboard, taking mental notes of the other swimmers' times. There's no one from Northern Hills in the D or C Finals. Maybe Andrews is right—maybe nothing holds back his swimmers.

As the B Final begins, I slip out of my parka, roll out my shoulders. Bouncing on my toes, I try to visualize the race, the feel of the water on my skin and the timer under my hand. Instead, the reporter's face materializes, the camera zooming in.

What about the possibility of having a seizure during the race?

My breath hitches; my heart rate spikes. I'm sprawled on the concrete, bleeding and struggling to make sense of my surroundings. Clouds of fear darken my thoughts, driven by a derecho of terrifying memories.

The whistle announces my heat. I know better than to look at anything other than the water, but I peer across the pool, spot Mac wrapped in a towel and nibbling on a power bar. Coach's arms are folded tight across her chest as she sways stiffly from side to side. Reporters cluck into cameras; I blink into the glare of a thousand screens.

If I have a seizure in the water, I might not be as lucky this time. I could drown while the entire country watches it happen.

My body bends forward, and my fingers grip the outer edge of the block. The starter pierces the air, and I take flight. As I surge through the water, my brain floats to a hospital room on the other side of the country. I smell bleach, see my parents' worried faces, hear their white lies. *Everything will be okay.*

When I break the surface at the end of the race, I know I didn't win.

55:02, the scoreboard announces in fluorescent numbers, just behind the first-place swimmer at 54:98.

"Nice swim," the girl next to me says. I turn toward her, ready to fend off the slap of sarcasm, but her face is kind, her smile genuine.

"You too," I mutter, heaving myself out of the water. I snatch up my towel and parka and hurry to the hospitality tent. Coach hovers at the edge of the pool, her eyes glued to the scoreboard. The A Final for the 100-meter free is starting, and Rachel will swim in the third heat.

Mac greets me on her way to the cooldown pool. "What happened?"

"I just kept thinking about what that reporter said. What if I had a seizure in the water again?"

200

Fear passes over Mac's face; then her jaw sets in resolve. "You're doing everything you're supposed to do. Between your meds and the lifeguards...You wouldn't be here if it wasn't safe. Right?"

"Right." I muster a thin smile, a failed attempt at reassurance.

The next whistle announces Rachel's heat. She flies into the water, flips into the second lap with precision, pulling ahead. Jealousy and pride mingle in my chest as I watch my fiercest competition take first place in her heat.

Coach bellows with pride. Mac cheers, jostling my shoulder as she jumps up and down. Rachel shoves up her goggles to scan the scoreboard; her fist pumps the air. I clap, thinking good for her, and also how badly I want to beat her in the 800-meter free.

As she climbs out of the pool, Coach's attention shifts to me. "You got in your head, didn't you?"

I nod.

"Your body is trained for this, Cooper. But I can't police your thoughts." Coach glances at her watch. "Whatever you need to do, do it now. You don't have much time before the 800."

Rachel joins me in the locker room, her earbuds in and her jaw fixed. I know she's already moved past her first win of the night, and is now zeroing in on her second.

"That was a good race," I tell her, changing into my distance suit. "Seriously—I was jealous."

Rachel grins.

As the A Final approaches, Coach gathers me and Rachel for a few last-minute words of advice. "Remember to pace yourself; reserve your strength."

"You've got this," Mac says, giving me a quick hug.

When the whistle announces our heat, I step onto the block, feel the familiar texture beneath my toes, and fix my eyes on the other end of the pool. The starter buzzes, and I dive in.

Like a dragonfly, hovering just above the surface, I watch my body go through the motions of freestyle: reach, pull, breathe. By the third lap, my muscles—tired from the 100-meter—begin to fatigue. Regret sings softly, growing louder with each stroke. Every ache, every throb reverberates throughout my body. The next time I come up for a breath, I catch a glimpse of the swimmer next to me, and I know she's pulling ahead.

Stay in the race. Looking at the other swimmers is the absolute worst thing to do, but I can't help it. This girl is one of the slowest in the heat. If she's a full length ahead of me, the fastest girls, including Rachel, have probably lapped me by now. The niggling voice at the back of my mind whispers that I'm going to lose anyway, so what's the point? My body carries me to the end of the race, but my brain checks out altogether.

By the time my hand touches the timer, the other swimmers are climbing out of the pool. Rachel shoots me a furious look. I hoist myself out of the water and storm toward the locker room, but not without catching the expression on Coach Andrews's face, lips turned up in disgust. Just like that, I know my future at Northern Hills is over before it began.

Coach Higgins steps in my path. "Tess, what—"

"Just don't." I push past her, skipping the snack and cooldown my body desperately needs. I pull sweats over my damp suit and shove out of the locker room, nearly bowling over the waiting reporter.

"Tess," she says. "You were a frontrunner for the 800-meter tonight. Can you tell us what happened out there?"

"No comment," I growl, elbowing past. I jog out of the arena, and flag down the first available shuttle.

I thought I belonged in the water. Turns out I don't belong anywhere at all.

"Get. Up."

Rachel's voice jerks me out of the dark relief of sleep. The lights are on in the hotel room, and she and Mac are standing over my bed, wearing bikinis and towels.

"We're going up to the hot tub," Mac says, hands firmly on her hips. "You're coming with us."

"I've had enough water for the day, thanks." I pull the pillow over my head.

Rachel yanks it off. "Enough with the melodrama. You represent Oakwood out there, and tonight you made us look bad."

"You weren't the one with the camera in your face!" I exclaim. "The only thing people like more than an underdog is a bloodbath, and mine was just broadcast to the entire country."

"Oh, get over yourself." Rachel tosses the pillow at me. "I'm going to the hot tub whether she comes or not."

"You should come," Mac says.

I reach for my phone, surprised to see it's only eight-thirty. Across town, the last event of the night is still underway. Three missed calls crowd my screen—two from my parents and one from Ali—but I can't face my family, not after I've let us all down.

"Fine, I'll go. Just give me a second to change."

The rooftop pool glows yellowish green, and the noise and lights of the city feel far away. A tired-looking dad flips through his phone and pretends to cheer every time his kid does a half-decent underwater handstand.

Steam rises as we ease into the hot water. It soothes my tense muscles, and I close my eyes, leaning back my neck against the edge.

Rachel flicks the surface, sending a spray of droplets at my face. "Are you going to tell us what the hell happened out there?"

"I don't really know," I admit. "Between those girls yesterday and that stupid reporter…" I tuck my knees against my chest; they stick out of the water like twin pale hills. "I should never have come this year."

"You're probably right," Rachel says.

"Rach!" Mac admonishes her with a splash, which Rachel immediately returns.

"I'm not talking about her seizures—God!" She wipes water out of her eyes. "I mean, you're not my favorite person, Tess."

"Wow," I grumble. "This pep talk is shaping up great."

"Would you shut up a second? Everybody already knows you're fast. But the thing that makes you dangerous is how bad you want the win. Tonight, you just let it slip right past you. You didn't even try."

I want to snap back at her, but she's right. I threw in the towel tonight, as if walking away on my own terms would somehow hurt less than trying my best and failing. Turns out self-inflicted pain isn't any easier to bear. Instead of being disappointed about a loss, I'm ashamed.

"I get that epilepsy is no joke," continues Rachel. "But if you lose your scholarship, that won't be the reason why."

"I don't know about that," I tell her. "Andrews was pissed tonight." The expression on my future coach's face after the 800-meter free looked exactly like Dad after Ali convinced him to buy the Nissan and the transmission blew the next day. Like he'd just realized he made a terrible investment. "He said nothing holds his swimmers back."

"Then show him nothing holds you back either," Rachel says.

I snort. "I'm pretty sure that ship has sailed."

"You still have the 200-meter free," Mac says.

"Don't remind me."

"Seriously," she pushes. "The 200 is your best event. It's a chance to remind Andrews why he offered you that scholarship in the first place."

"Just don't crap out," Rachel says. "It's no fun to beat you when you don't try."

I splash her, and Mac cracks up. And I wonder if Rachel's right—maybe it's not epilepsy that's ruining my life. Maybe it's me.

———

"Hey," I say into the phone. I'm tucked between the cool hotel sheets, the blanket pulled up to my chin.

"Hey, kid." Dad's voice is a soft growl in my ear. He doesn't ask how I'm feeling—he already knows. His breath whispers into the receiver as he waits for me to speak.

"I embarrassed us," I say, nearly choking on the words. "I'm so sorry." I don't know if I'm apologizing to him or to myself.

"What's the only thing I've ever asked of you?" Dad's coaching voice is so familiar, my chest aches.

"Do my best," I whisper.

"That's exactly right. After everything you've been through this summer, just showing up makes you a hero in my book," he says. "But this isn't about me, or your mom, or even your scholarship. This is about you and what you want."

Tears cling to my lashes. Tonight, my dreams were so close I could taste them, and I turned around and walked away.

"You do your best—whatever that looks like—and you'll always be a winner to me," Dad says.

I promise him I will, but as I sink into my pillow, I replay the words. Is my best good enough for the world of competitive swimming? Is it good enough for me? The question lingers, playing out in my dreams.

CHAPTER
TWENTY-SEVEN

Coach is pacing the lobby in the morning when I join the rest of my team to meet the shuttle. "It's about time!" she exclaims. "You ready?"

"I hope so." Even if I can't measure up to Coach Andrews's expectations, at least I'll show him I have heart.

Coach steers me toward the shuttle. "You took a big gamble showing up this year," she says. "I'm not sure I would've been able to do it."

I gape at her. "You gave me so much crap about quitting!"

"It's my job to get the best out of my team. And your best, Tess, blows me away. You've barely touched the edges of your potential. I just couldn't let that go to waste."

"Clearly you missed last night's race."

She shrugs off my sarcasm. "This morning's a new start. Don't pay any attention to the other teams. And stay far away from Wes Andrews."

"Got it."

"It's just you and the water," Coach says, as we climb into the shuttle. "Today nothing else matters."

Mac and Rachel flank my sides like bodyguards as we walk into the arena, ready to throat punch any Northern Hills girls that dare to step in our path. I keep my eyes straight ahead and my earbuds in, avoiding any stray glimpses of Coach Andrews.

The 200-meter free is one of the first preliminary races, and Rachel and I warm up together, then head to the locker room to change before the first heat begins.

"You're quiet this morning," Rachel says, squinting at me in the mirror as she snaps her swim cap into place.

"Just trying to focus."

"Good."

My phone buzzes—a FaceTime call from Charlie—and my heart lurches into my throat. I turn my back to the lockers to answer. Charlie's face materializes, with Howie at the kitchen table in the background. A few boxes are stacked against the wall behind him.

"Hey, this isn't actually a great time," I say. "I'm about to—"

"I know," Charlie says. "But I just wanted to show you what we're working on." He turns the phone around as Howie holds up a giant piece of posterboard, decorated in markers and glitter: TEAM SUNSHINE.

"We're all ready for tonight," Charlie says, turning the phone back around. "We've got the popcorn to throw, and you know, probably eat, and the TV completely reserved. Even though we can't be there in person, your cheering section is getting amped."

My chest squeezes, and tears sting my eyes. "Thanks, guys."

"No biggie," Charlie says. "I only ever bet on a sure thing."

I end the call, a smile stretching to my ears, and crank up my race music on the way out to the pool. The swimmers in the first heat of the 200-meter free are readying themselves behind the blocks.

Nerves crawl across my skin like ants. In this race, more than any other, swimmers find out what they're made of, and the full weight of that is heavy on my shoulders this morning. I shake out my arms, desperate to clear the mounting pressure. As the second heat takes the blocks, I'm debating between barfing and catching the first shuttle back to the hotel. Instead, I slip out of my parka and get in line with the rest of the third-heat swimmers. *One race at a time.* This will be over in two minutes. For two minutes, I can show up.

When the whistle announces my heat, I lower my goggles and step up onto the block, granting myself one sideways glance at Rachel. She breaks her focus long enough to nod: *You've got this.* There's no time to wonder if she's right because the starter buzzes, and my body breaks the water's surface.

Reach. Pull. Breathe.

In the first lap, I remember what it felt like to swim when I was younger—how I pushed fearlessly out into the water, oblivious to what it could take from me. I belonged in it, like a fish or a mermaid. Now, I'm learning to swim all over again.

My chest begins to burn in the second lap. The girl next to me picks up speed, edging past, and I know my best isn't going to be good enough to place. This summer—for all its challenges—has shaped me, more than any race I've ever won. My friendship with Mac, stronger where it's healed. My family, imperfect but steadfast. And Charlie, the boy who loves me for being myself.

Midway through the third lap, and another swimmer's toes ripple just past my fingertips. I reach for them, not to prove anything to anyone. But because no matter how my life has changed, the water has carried me through it all. For these two minutes and for as long as I can, I'm going to show up to the sport I love. I'm going to live into the person I've been all along, the person epilepsy can't take away.

As I roll into the fourth lap, my body explodes.

I feel everything and nothing.

I am not a fish.

I am not a mermaid.

I am the water.

My hand slams the buzzer, and I heave upward with a gasping breath. The first thing I see is Mac on her toes, screaming and punching the air. The second is Coach, who flings her arms around Mac, leaving her speechless. And the third is the clock.

1:58:69.

I made the A final, second in the heat—a breath ahead of Rachel.

I lean forward, shouting to Rachel across the lanes between us, my words full of gratitude. "Nice try!"

"It's about time you showed up," she hollers.

Coach meets us at the edge of the pool. "Great swim," she says, clapping both of us on our wet shoulders. And then, wasting no time, "Now you just have to do it again tonight."

"Thanks, Coach," I say.

"Hurry up and go grab something to eat."

Rachel and I head toward the hospitality tent, Mac practically skipping alongside us. I'm unwrapping my bar and heading to the cooldown pool when Coach Andrews stops me.

"Cooper," he says, a stern look on his face.

"Coach?"

"That's the way you swim for me every single time. It's always all or nothing."

A chunk of bar lodges in my throat. "Does this mean I'm still on the team?"

Andrews nods. "As long as I don't ever see you swim like you did yesterday again. Got it?"

"Yes, sir," I say, knees soft with relief.

"Did I just hear what I think I did?" Rachel asks.

"I'm still on the team," I tell them, though Andrews's words felt far less than congratulatory.

"I bet he's pissed you beat one of his girls," Mac says.

"Did I?"

As we head to the cooldown pool, Mac fills us in on the race, our best moments, and the final thrilling seconds, when Rachel and I swam mere millimeters apart.

"Just wait until the 100-meter relay tomorrow," Rachel says with a sly smile. "The three of us will really put on a show."

———

The reporter is waiting for me after the 200-meter free A Final tonight. I tear myself away from my phone, blowing up with congratulatory texts from my family, Charlie, and even a few people from group. While my final time wasn't nearly as good as my preliminary race this morning, I'm confident I did my best and proud of the way I represented my team.

"You had quite the comeback today," the reporter says. "What's the secret?"

"I just did my best," I say, knowing Dad's watching and will hear the meaning in my words. "I'm so glad I get to be here to compete."

The reporter's eyes drop to my shirt, thrown on after the race for this exact reason. I stretch out the purple fabric so the camera can clearly see the numbers: 1 IN 26. "It's the number of people who could develop epilepsy in their lifetime," I say. "It's much more common than you think, but most people don't know anything about it. I'm not the first contender with epilepsy—hopefully, I won't be the last."

"I thought you didn't want people to know you had epilepsy," Mac says as the reporter moves on to Rachel.

I hook my arm in hers and tug her close. "Turns out I do."

CHAPTER
TWENTY-EIGHT

Three days later, I'm waiting in the airport, enjoying a well-deserved caramel Frap and rehashing the week's exhilarating highs and crushing lows along with the rest of my team. We're all exhausted after an incredible end to the season and looking forward to a few precious days of recovery before a new season begins. For many of us, this coming year will be our last at Oakwood, before we head out into the world to swim with a new team for a new coach.

The intercom crackles, and the gate attendant announces we'll be boarding in a few minutes. "I have to pee," Mac says, handing me her coffee and standing up.

"Me too," says Rachel.

"Me three," says Simone.

"You coming?" Rachel asks.

"I'm good."

As the girls head off to the bathroom, I take out my phone. I've been in constant communication with Charlie, my family, and people from group. Ali says Mom tipped over a plate of nachos during the 200-meter free, and she plans to never let her live it down. Chris offered me a T-shirt sponsorship, payment in the already-free cookies Ian brings.

"Tess Cooper?" A man's voice jerks me out of my thoughts. Gray streaks his dark brown hair, and I vaguely recognize the team emblem on his jacket. "Tom Kirk," he says, sticking out his hand. "I coach the team at Center Valley."

Center Valley—a small college a few hours north of Oakwood. Over the last week, a handful of Center Valley swimmers placed with great time. I stand up and shake his hand. "You guys had a nice showing this week."

"You did, too," he says with a smile. "I hope you don't mind me saying so, but I heard about your health challenges. Not too many people would show up after that. And even fewer would come back from a rough first night. I was really impressed."

Pride blooms in my chest, and my neck gets hot. "Thanks, Coach."

Over Kirk's shoulder, I see Coach Higgins watching our conversation. She sees me notice and glances away.

"Listen," Kirk says. "I hear you're headed to Northern Hills, but I want you to know you've got a spot on my team if you're interested, no matter what happens with your health."

"Seriously?"

He nods. "Swimmers with heart are more important to me than swimmers with natural talent. And you have both. It's a win-win in my book."

I tell the coach I'll consider his offer; we shake hands again before he heads back to his team. One of the girls swam next to me in the 100-meter free B Finals. When I make eye contact with her, she smiles and waves.

"So?" Coach Higgins says, suddenly standing right next to me.

"Like you didn't already hear everything."

She smirks. "I missed a few words. Fill me in."

I tell her about Kirk's offer, a surreal feeling settling over me as I replay his words.

"He's got a good team and an incredible facility," Coach Higgins says. "And I've heard they prioritize inclusion. He'd take good care of you."

"You think so?"

She smiles at me. "I do."

My family is waiting for me at baggage claim. They enclose me in a giant group hug, and I hold on for a few extra seconds just to breathe them in. On the way home, we stop for dinner at Dad's favorite burger joint, and I fill them in on every second of the last week. Mom lights up when I tell her about Coach Kirk's offer. She's always wanted me to go to a school where I didn't have to swim for my keep. Dad and I want a school that will help me pursue my athletic dreams. None of us ever thought we could have it both ways.

I fall asleep on the way home, jerking awake when we pull into the driveway. While Dad grabs my luggage out of the trunk, I climb out of the van and stretch. This is the same house where I've always lived, the same road where I stood last week. Yet it all seems different now. I'm different now. The past few months have shown me that life doesn't always turn out the way you planned. And if my plan means always striving for perfection and coming up short, then it might be time for a new one.

"You coming?" Ali asks, wheeling my suitcase toward the door.

And that's when I see it: a U-Haul heading past our house with Charlie at the wheel.

I don't answer Ali. I just take off running.

Because I don't need to know what the future holds anymore. I just want to show up.

I trail the U-Haul, waving and shouting. The brake lights flash; the truck shudders as it comes to a halt.

Charlie climbs out of the front seat, bewilderment plain on his face. "What are you doing?"

It takes me a second to recalibrate. I smooth back hair that clings to my cheek, realizing I probably smell like airplane peanuts and sweat.

But I don't care. Charlie's leaving, and I'm never going to let something good slip through my fingers again.

"I just...you're leaving," I stumble.

"Yeah," Charlie says, glancing back at the U-Haul. "Taking out my mom's stuff for her."

"I just wanted to say—" I blink, realization dawning. "Your mom's stuff?"

Charlie puts his hands in his pockets and looks at the sky over my shoulder. It's deep gray with streaks of orange and pink, like poppies, like possibility.

"She and Max moved out this weekend. But I decided I'm going to hang out here for a while." He squints at me. "Try and figure out what I want, you know? Maybe you can help me make a plan."

My body flickers like a thousand fireflies. "Plans aren't always what they're cracked up to be."

"No?"

I step closer, wind my fingers around the back of his neck, and press my lips to his. I don't know what's ahead for us, and I don't need to. I trust we'll figure it out together.

Charlie wraps me against his chest and holds me tight. It feels like being underwater, encompassed by warmth and undulating light and the otherworldly feeling of being exactly where I belong. My life beckons—full of everything I love and all that I am.

I dive in.

ACKNOWLEDGMENTS

Like Tess, I tend to be a planner. I love my calendar, to-do list, and long-term goals. And while those tools can be helpful guides to launch a project or journey, I've found the most important elements of a good plan are flexibility and grace. My grandmother (a Southern Baptist preacher's wife and lifelong writer) has been known to say, "If you want to make God laugh, make a plan." This has never been truer in my life than when I was diagnosed with epilepsy in my thirties. This diagnosis—and the everyday miracles of community, creativity, and faith that I have learned to lean on because of it—has taught me that the path unfolds as we walk it, and that, sometimes, broken roads lead to beautiful places.

This book has so much of my heart in it, and so many incredible people have helped bring it to fruition. The thriving teenagers and young adults from the Epilepsy Foundation of Eastern Pennsylvania helped inspire and inform Tess's story. Aly (Ackman) Synnestvedt provided a wealth of knowledge on the complicated world of competitive swimming, with which I took much creative license. Any oversimplification, exclusions, or errors are my own.

I owe a huge debt of gratitude to my early readers, particularly Chrissa Pederson, critique partner extraordinaire. You are the antidote to procrastination and creative meltdown—thank you for saving me from myself (over and over again). Thank you to my army of fierce friends who cheer me on and pick me up. Thank you to Laura and Della for believing in Tess's story and for helping her shine.

To Scott, Caitlyn, and Charlotte: Thank you for walking this broken road with me. You have always been my Plan A.

ABOUT THE AUTHOR

Abbey Nash holds an MA in English from Arcadia University. She lives with her husband and two daughters outside of Philadelphia, where she works as a senior marketing writer in the healthcare industry. A former writing teacher, she enjoys leading creative writing workshops and has presented at SCBWI events and the National Council of Teachers of English, as well as at local schools and universities. When she's not writing or talking about writing, you can find her reading, spending time with her family, or walking her highly opinionated Australian Shepherd. *Breathing Underwater* is her second novel.